I0456864

NO CHOICE

DEBORAH WALLACE

Choice Series: No Choice

Published by Deborah Wallace

Copyright © 2021 by Deborah Wallace

ISBN 978-1-951457-12-9

10/23, 8/24

Cover Art by Raymond and Deborah Wallace

All rights reserved.
This book is a work of fiction. All names, characters, places and
incidents are either the product of the author's imagination or
are used fictitiously. Any resemblance to actual persons, events
or places is coincidental. No part of this book may be repro-
duced in any form by electronic or mechanical means, including
information storage and retrieval systems, without written per-
mission from the author, except for the use of brief quotations
in a book review.

Chapter 1

Theo Argyle strode past the hostess with a wave—beautiful, but certainly not Jessalyn with her blue eyes and blonde hair that he wanted to take down from her customary ponytail. He had a standing Friday reservation at Zentaro's Restaurant for the same table in Jessalyn's section. After talking and joking with her for the last six months, he was ready to ask her out. He'd been fighting his growing attraction, but had given in when he discovered she wasn't as young as he thought.

He never used his business credit card to pay for dining because it had his title of CEO on it. As the major shareholder of AAJ Electronics, he was afraid he'd intimidate her, and although she wouldn't likely be after his money, he didn't want it to influence their early relationship.

A few tables over from where he threaded his way through, three men caught his attention when Jessalyn's name was mentioned. One was Mitch Waters, a man he'd unfortunately lent money to for a business idea. Theo got a bad vibe from the other men. He stopped on the opposite of a column and watched.

The man to Mitch's right must lift weights regularly to get those massive muscles. His silent scrutiny of Mitch made Theo think the man might be a bodyguard.

The last man had a touch of gray at his temples and intimidation radiated off him. His wide shoulders and lack of fat showed he took care of himself.

1

"Mr. Mansard, I don't have all the money right now." Mitch's voice shook.

A chill passed through Theo. Jessalyn should be no part of this conversation, not with a man like Mansard. Theo's stepfather Gary, a police detective, had worked on some murder cases that implicated Mansard, but nothing could be tied to the man. He was known in some circles as a loan shark and pimp.

Mansard leaned toward Mitch. "Your full payment was due last week. You know I don't like late payments."

Mitch rubbed his forehead. "I already told you I don't have fifty grand. I can continue paying installments."

Mansard jabbed a finger on the table in front of Mitch. Without raising his voice, it somehow still sounded more menacing. "That's not the deal you signed. Payment in full by the thirtieth of this month. There are three ways to clear your debt. Pay the money immediately, do a few jobs for me…"

He could mean any number of things Theo wouldn't want to do. Considering the man's reputation, Mitch might have to commit a murder, beat up someone, or steal for Mansard.

"Or give me your sister."

Mitch fisted his hands on the table. "I can't give you Jessalyn. She's not my property."

Theo's stomach clenched. He hadn't known the man he'd lent money to was related to Jessalyn. If Mansard got his hands on her, her life would be brutally over. She might not die right away, but she'd be better off if she did. She could end up like the murdered women in his stepfather's cases. Maybe he should call Gary, but would the detective arrive in time? Business might be concluded and Jessalyn gone by then.

Theo hated the idea of any young girl being forced into prostitution, and Jessalyn more than any other.

Mansard tisked. "Do you think I'd hurt that pretty little thing? She's more valuable to me as she is."

Mitch blanched. "I, ah. How long would she be with you?"

Mansard lifted a corner of his mouth and rubbed his chin. "I'll give her back after a year."

Theo strode to the table and dropped his hand on Mitch's shoulder. "Excuse me. I need to speak with Mitch."

Mitch stared up at Theo.

Mansard glared. "You're interrupting a business transaction."

"Now!" Theo squeezed Mitch's shoulder hard.

The bodyguard rose a couple of inches, but Mansard shook his head.

Theo led Mitch outside. "Do you know what that man plans to do with your sister? He'll put her on the street as a hooker. In a year, she'll be an empty shell."

Mitch paled again. "He said he wouldn't hurt her."

Theo couldn't believe how naïve this man was, or purposely blind. "Yeah? He'll let the johns do that, but he'll get her hooked on drugs. Do you really want to do that to your sister?"

Mitch covered his mouth and ran to the edge of the walk then threw up into the bushes. He wiped his mouth with the back of his hand. "I don't know what to do."

"A brave man would take responsibility for his own mess and not force his sister to pay for it. But I'll help you out. I have an alternate proposition. I'll pay your debt."

"But I owe him fifty-thousand."

"I'll also forgive the hundred-thousand you owe me, but your sister comes with me." The words about Jessalyn left his mouth before he realized what he was saying. In his head, he'd offered to pay the debt to protect her, but it wasn't what he said.

Theo didn't trust Mitch to stay out of trouble. It couldn't be helped, but Mitch was getting off without even a slap on the wrist. Now that Mitch knew he could turn his sister over for payment, it would be easier to trade her again. Theo wouldn't give him the chance.

Mitch frowned. "You'll treat her right?"

3

Theo stepped closer. "What does it matter to you? You were going to give her to a monster."

Mitch turned red. "I didn't have a choice with him."

Theo almost punched Mitch. "You had the choice of doing 'a few jobs' which probably means some of his illegal dirty work. Instead, you chose to turn your sister over to him, leaving yourself unscathed." Theo couldn't imagine doing that to his little sister. "Since you refuse to man up and take that choice, here are your choices. Sell her to Mansard. She'll be forced to become a prostitute and probably die in a year, and you'll still owe me a hundred thousand." He paused to let the message sink in. "Or you bring her to me, and I'll keep her safe."

Mitch let out a long breath. "All right."

Mitch couldn't know Theo wasn't like Mansard, and didn't seem to care as long as his mistakes were covered over.

"And." Theo poked a finger into Mitch's chest. "Do not borrow money again or you'll regret it." He still seethed at this man's lack of responsibility. "Let's go back inside and finish this."

He strode up to Mansard's table and stood over the man. "I'm paying what Mitch Water's owes you. I'll do a bank transfer right now, and you can write paid on his debt."

The man crossed his arms. "I don't want someone else involved in this arrangement. I happen to like the deal I have with Waters." He'd probably planned on getting Jessalyn all along.

Mansard stared at Theo for a good two minutes—probably trying to figure out Theo's angle and if this was the best deal he could get. He'd likely earn more than fifty grand pimping Jessalyn out, and now that he'd been so close to getting her, he didn't want to back down.

Mansard grinned. "You can pay off Water's debt and have Jessalyn for sixty thousand."

With the money Theo had already committed to rescuing

Jessalyn, the extra ten thousand was nothing. "Done."

Theo hoped it was done. Mansard could have been plotting something more in all the time he took to give his response. Jessalyn still might not be safe.

"Fine." Mansard snapped his fingers. "Ricko, give the man the account number for the transfer."

Ricko showed Theo the number on his cell phone, and Theo used his own phone to enter it into his bank account and put through the transfer.

Mansard pulled out his phone and smiled. The transfer must have shown up already. He wrote on a paper, took a picture of it then thrust the page at Mitch. Theo snatched it away and studied it. 'Paid' was scrawled on a loan document with a date and Mansard's signature.

Theo tucked it in his pocket, and eyed Mitch. There was no way he'd let Mitch hold the receipt. "Let me know if he gives you any trouble over this." Theo grabbed Mitch's arm and dragged him away from Mansard's table. "Bring Jessalyn and her luggage to my house at ten tomorrow." He wrote his address on the back of a business card and handed it to him.

Theo wouldn't want to be in Mitch's shoes when he told Jessalyn what he'd done to her. At the moment, Theo didn't want to be in his own shoes.

He headed to his car. His stomach churned, his appetite gone, and he couldn't face Jessalyn tonight. He climbed into the seat and punched the steering wheel. This night was supposed to end with a date set up with Jessalyn, not forcing her to come to him. He would put off facing her until morning.

~~~

At the end of the evening, Jessalyn Waters dashed to her brother's car and got in. She kicked off her shoes and tipped the seat back a couple notches before buckling her seatbelt. Fridays were her favorite day to work because Mr. Argyle came in and sat in her section. He'd been coming in for months and must have had every item on the dinner menu. His favorite was manicotti, if how often he ordered it meant anything.

Every time she passed his table, she'd stop and they'd talk for a few minutes. More recently, she made sure she passed it often. Those penetrating brown eyes seemed to see straight into her, and she wondered what it would be like to kiss him. There'd been more than once she had to stop herself from running her fingers through his deep brown, wavy hair.

She sighed. Since the first time she saw him, he hadn't missed a Friday—until tonight. He probably had a date and wouldn't bring her to a place where he flirted with a server. Her whole evening had been dismal.

Jessalyn hadn't realized Mitch had been as silent as her until they arrived home, neither having uttered a word. She squeezed his arm. "Hey, Mitch. Is something bothering you?"

He blew out a breath, grimaced, and got out of the car.

She collected her shoes and purse then went inside barefoot.

Mitch paced in the kitchen. She'd never seen him like this, not even when Bridget broke up with him after they'd dated for two years. She hoped he hadn't gotten fired from his job.

Jessalyn stepped in his path and grabbed his biceps. "What is wrong with you?"

His expression reminded her of when he'd told her their parents had died. Nothing could be as bad as that.

She shook him. "Talk to me!"

He shrugged out of her grasp and put his hands on his head, fisting his hair. "Jess…"

"Mitch! What? You're scaring me."

He spun away then turned back to her. "I sold you!"

She gaped. No way he said what she thought he said. "Say that again."

"I. Sold. You."

6

Her whole body instantly went cold. "You can't do that. People can't do that." He had to mean something else. "Do you mean you volunteered my time for something?"

"No, Jess. I owed this guy a hundred K, and I didn't have it to pay him back. So he's taking you as payment."

"No! Mitch, you wouldn't do that to me." She rammed the heels of her hands into his chest. Mitch, No!"

He grabbed her wrists. "I'm sorry."

Jessalyn couldn't remember a time she'd been more angry or hurt. After the long evening without her favorite customer, she'd wanted to relax when she got home then go to bed, but Mitch's news destroyed her life. It had been them against the world for eight years. He didn't *just* throw her away, he profited from getting rid of her. "You sold me? My own brother sold me as if I was a slave!" She yanked her arms out of his hands.

"Jess, it's not like that!"

She dropped her hands to her hips. "Really? You owed the man a hundred grand. To settle the debt, you *gave* me to him. How is it not selling me?" She turned her back, not able to look at the brother who'd betrayed her. Her breath sawed in and out. She'd read about women being kidnapped and sold into sexual slavery but never expected she'd be in such a position. It was Mitch's problem. She'd refuse to go.

He touched her shoulder. She shrugged it off and spun around.

He rubbed a hand across his mouth. "I'm sorry. I didn't have a choice."

She propped her hands on her hips. "Really? That was the only option? 'Pay up or give me your sister?'"

His gaze dropped. "I feared for my life."

"What about the police?"

Mitch frantically shook his head. "We can't call. I'm dead if we go to them."

"And there's nothing else you can do?"

He clenched his hands. "I don't have the money to pay it

back."

"Mitch, since Mom and Dad died, you've been my rock. You were still in high school and kept us out of foster homes." Tears streamed down her cheeks. "It was us against the world, and now you're trading me for a debt. We could have come up with something. We always do."

"I should have talked to you about it, but now it's too late."

If a man had stood in front of them and said Mitch would die completing some dangerous task, but she could save him by giving herself to someone, she would have done it. Now, she was in that position without her consent. She wanted to rebel but worried it would cost Mitch his life.

"When are you supposed to hand me over?"

"I have to take you to his house tomorrow morning."

"What's..." Like it mattered who the man was. He'd probably expect her to call him Master.

Jessalyn packed her suitcase and shoved her clothes in Mitch's bag, too. When those were filled, she grabbed a trash bag and stuffed in her shoes, then her remaining clothes. On top, she placed some mementos she couldn't live without—pictures of her parents, books, and a stuffed dog.

If she somehow wiggled out of being this man's property, she wouldn't return to the apartment with Mitch. He didn't deserve a sister.

Chapter 2

Promptly at ten in the next day, Jessalyn sat beside Mitch in his car as he turned into the driveway of a mansion—two stories and more windows than she had time to count. Would she live here, or would the buyer take her to some sleazy place to hide her?

If she did live here, she'd have to find out where the nearest bus stop was so she could get to school and work. There wouldn't be one in this neighborhood. If she was allowed to leave the house. Maybe he'd keep her a prisoner.

He might be a violent man. If Mitch feared him, she might have reason to also. She'd worried through the night, but now that she was moments from facing her future, she began to tremble.

Mitch grabbed one suitcase and the trash bag. Jessalyn got out and gripped the door while she bucked up her courage to go through with this. Once her limbs were steadier, she tossed her backpack full of school books and laptop over her shoulder and rolled the remaining bag. They walked up the front steps, and Mitch rang the doorbell. Jessalyn stood behind him, her hand clamped on her bag. She had no idea what would be expected of her.

She let the anger at Mitch and her worry for his life override the fear of what her life would become. It was the only thing keeping her standing or from bursting into tears.

The door opened and Mr. Argyle stood there in a suit. Her

heart plunged into her stomach and rolled over. She expected to see someone who looked like a criminal, not the man who was the subject of all her fantasies. That dark hair, long enough to run her fingers through, those brown eyes, warm enough to melt her. His smile and kind words made her Fridays brighter. He was always nice to all the staff, but maybe it was all show to hide a dark underside.

He might not be the one who bought her, but if not, he was helping that person. She'd never have thought he'd stoop to buying someone. Another shock hit when she wondered if she might not be the first one.

Today, there was no smile, and he had shadows under his eyes.

Jessalyn wondered if he'd get her settled and go into the office. Maybe he'd lock her up so she couldn't run away.

He barely glanced at her. "Come into the dining room. Mitch, I have papers for you to sign."

They set their bags in the foyer and followed Mr. Argyle. She noticed for the first time how tall he was. She'd only ever been close to him when he was seated. He was at least four inches taller than Mitch, and she'd never thought of her brother as short.

Mr. Argyle patted some papers on the table, a beautiful mahogany. "Look these over. Initial the first page and sign the last."

Someone must have dropped her into the seventeenth century. Her brother signed her over to this man, and she wasn't expected to do anything on her behalf.

She glared at the papers as her brother read through them. They couldn't actually say she was sold property. If that came to light, Mr. Argyle would be in trouble, and she doubted he was a fool.

"Well, um. I'll see you soon, Jess." Mitch hugged her, but she stood stiff.

She trailed behind as they returned to the front door, and Mitch left.

Now, she was alone with a stranger. A few days ago, she wouldn't have considered him as such. She didn't know much about him, but had liked his personality from all the times they chatted at Zentaro's. This fiasco proved he wasn't the man she thought he was.

Mr. Argyle ran a hand through his hair. He wasn't as calm now that Mitch was gone. Good. He deserved to squirm. "I think we should get married."

"What?" She couldn't have heard right. "Mr. Argyle, did you say *married*?" Her heart pounded and she clutched a hand to her chest. She should be relegated to a dungeon with a big bed so she could accommodate his every whim.

"Call me Theo. Yes. You're—"

"You bought a bride, not a slave? Wouldn't it have been cheaper to ask me out and see where it went?"

He slipped his hands into his pockets. "I *was* planning on asking you out. Last night, in fact. But when I got to Zentaro's—"

"You were at Zentaro's last night?" No one had told her they'd seen him.

"Yes. Mitch was there, and I overheard him talking to George Mansard and—"

"Who's that?" This whole situation was bizarre. With Theo seeming uncomfortable, she regained a bit of courage.

He gestured toward the living room as big as her whole apartment. "Maybe we better sit down for this." He strode to the doorway and turned, waiting for her.

This had to be bad. She thought she'd already experienced bad, but if she needed to sit, it had to be worse. She took a shaky breath and followed him.

He sat on the far end of the couch, and she dropped down on the opposite end, sinking into the buttery soft leather.

Theo rubbed a hand over his mouth. "Mansard is a pimp

and loan shark. Didn't Mitch tell you about him?"

She shook her head. "No. He only said he traded me for his debt to you."

Theo grimaced. "Well, he did owe me a hundred thousand—" his gaze dropped "—that I would have written off at the end of the year anyway." He looked her in the eye. "But he owed money to Mansard, too. Fifty thousand. Mansard gave Mitch an option of repayment or doing some jobs, which he rejected. Instead, he chose to give you to Mansard."

"Then how come I'm with you?"

He slid to the center cushion and lightly gripped her upper arms, putting his face a foot from hers. "Mansard would've made you a prostitute. He likely would have had you turning your first trick last night. I couldn't let that happen, so I stepped in and paid what Mitch owed and ten thousand more."

Jessalyn's shoulders sagged. If she'd been standing, she would have hit the floor. Her brother was handing her to a pimp. She thought she'd be one man's sex slave, which was bad enough, but being passed around and used had to be ten times worse. If Theo hadn't come in when he did, she'd be violated already and maybe beaten for fighting back.

He placed a hand over hers. It felt hot because hers was so cold. "When that evil man said your name, I would have done anything to keep you out of his hands. I didn't have time to think. I marched up to the table and told Mitch I'd take you instead. I convinced Mansard to take the money from me, and I forgave Mitch the hundred grand he owed me."

The concern in his face, the gentle hand on hers, and that scent from her daydreams, all combined into a twisted mess with the fact he'd *paid* someone for her. If he was to be believed, he'd paid to keep her out of the hands of a pimp—in this instance, protecting her better than her brother.

"Was Mitch's life in danger doing those jobs?"

Theo shrugged. "It might have been. I have no idea what

Mansard would make him do."

Jessalyn was mad all over again at Mitch. "So he traded the possibility of him getting injured or killed with the sure thing I'd be raped and…whatever else." She didn't want to think about it.

Surely, Theo must feel something for her to willingly lose a hundred-sixty thousand dollars. "But why get married?"

"I figure if we're married, Mitch can't sell you again, and Mansard will give up."

If she refused his offer, she wouldn't move back in with Mitch. Not after the way he betrayed her. "I can move in with a girlfriend." At least until she found her own place. Or more likely, someone needing a roommate.

He shook his head. "Then you're basically alone. Exactly the situation that Mansard preys on all the time. You were almost his and I snatched you away. Now, he may have set his sights on you."

She'd rather go back to being a nobody this Mansard guy had never seen. She didn't know if marriage was necessary to protect her, but Theo felt so strongly about it he was giving up his freedom as well as all that money. She didn't understand his motive.

Was accepting his offer of marriage a choice, or no choice since it appeared to be her only option to stay safe?

Theo helped her to stand. Her legs wobbled.

She focused on his tie. "Okay. I'll marry you."

He blew out a breath. "Can you change into a pretty dress? We have an appointment with the judge at noon."

Her gaze flew to his face. "You knew I'd say yes?"

He pinched his lips together.

"You weren't going to let me say no?"

"I don't think I should answer that."

Jessalyn tipped her head. "Yeah. You probably shouldn't."

Her life had been turned upside down. Sometime today she'd be married to a man she barely knew. It sure beat being forced into prostitution. She couldn't imagine Theo Argyle would make her a prostitute after marrying her.

She stared at her bags, packed in haste. Which one held something semi-appropriate to get married in? Everything she brought with her probably cost less than the price of his suit. He put himself in this position, he'd get whatever she could find. She drew in a long breath and stiffened her back. "Where do I change?"

"Oh. This way." He picked up her suitcases and bags except her backpack and headed for the stairs. Halfway up, the stairs divided, with narrower sets going right and left. Theo headed left and pointed up the other stairs. "Susan, Gary, and Autumn live in that wing."

In the upper hallway, doors lined both sides. Theo tapped the second one on the right. "This is Bradley's room." They passed two more pairs of doors before stepping into the open doorway at the end. He continued through a living room and into another room then set all the bags on a king-size bed.

It was a masculine room. Dark wood floor and dark furniture, tan drapes, and cream walls. A few personal items sat on a dresser. This was Theo's room.

Cold radiated from her chest into the rest of her body. Sex slave to... married sex slave? After they got married, he might expect sex by this afternoon. She found him attractive, and for months she'd had fantasies about him, but not like this.

"This is your room? Are you expecting me to sleep in here with you?"

She almost laughed at his blush. He wasn't as cool as he appeared.

"We're not having sex yet."

But he expected it at some point. At least she could put that off. For tonight. She dropped her fists on her hips and narrowed her eyes. "When exactly does that end?"

He looked her in the eye. "When we know each other better, and you decide you want to have sex. I hope someday you'll come to feel the same way about me as I already do toward you."

That was a huge weight off her chest. Almost everything he did showed he cared about her. She hoped it was true.

He checked his watch. "I'll leave you to get changed. We still have to stop by the jewelers for our rings."

Wedding rings. The door closed behind him. At least he wasn't staying to watch her change.

Jessalyn pulled out her ancient phone and called her brother. She thought she'd never talk to him again, but she needed to verify what Theo told her.

"Jess? Are you okay?"

"So far. No thanks to you. Were you going to sell me to a pimp named Mansard, and Theo Argyle stopped you?"

"Jess, I—"

She raised her voice. "That's a yes or no question."

"Yes, but—"

"So, fearing for your life was because of this Mansard guy and not Mr. Argyle?"

"Yes. I don't think Mr. Argyle will hurt you."

"You didn't think if you feared for your life maybe I should fear for mine?"

"I didn't think about that. I'm so sorry, Jess."

"Not sorry enough." She ended the call. Maybe Theo Argyle *had* saved Mitch's life. He'd certainly saved her from being thrown to the pimp wolves.

Jessalyn shook herself. She never imagined she would marry a near stranger. In her imagined wedding, Mitch would have walked her down the aisle, but she didn't want to see him—maybe ever again.

Her life had changed, and she didn't know yet if it was for better or worse. Like in wedding vows.

~~~

15

No Choice

Theo paced in his sitting room. He rarely used this space. Most often, he watched movies in the first floor living room, and was often joined by Bradley, Autumn, Susan or Gary. His stepmother was more like a sister since she was only five years older than him, more so since his dad died. Gary had fit well into the household after he and Susan married. Bradley jokingly called him their quasi-brother-in-law.

It would probably be best if he and Jessalyn spent time together in the sitting room, getting to know each other away from the family. It would be obvious to them he and Jessalyn didn't know each other well, and they'd wonder why he'd jumped into marriage with her. That was a question *he* didn't know the answer to either.

He hadn't given her a choice, not really. From the moment he'd overheard her name in Zentaro's, he'd needed to protect her. All those evenings of snatched conversations had embedded her into his heart. He'd raced to her rescue and couldn't back down from that. He hated taking away her choices, but having spent half the night thinking about the whole situation, he wouldn't have done anything differently. He hoped she'd forgive him.

Theo glanced at his watch. Jessalyn was taking too long. Maybe she'd changed her mind. She had to cooperate for a wedding to take place.

The door opened and Jessaylyn hovered in the doorway. She was breathtaking.

He'd only ever seen her in her server dress or pants, and the jeans and shirt she arrived in, but now she wore a knee-length, white dress with tiny pink flowers on it. The ponytail her blonde hair had always been in was replaced with cascading curls around her shoulders. Her eyes and cheeks were complimented with a bit of color.

He ached to hug her, but held back, not wanting to scare her. Their first kiss would be in front of the judge at the wedding, and their wedding night would not include sex. He'd never imagined himself in this kind of predicament, but there was no way he could back down.

"You're beautiful." Reflexively, he held his hand out to her, and wished he hadn't. She might reject his spontaneous action, although, her changing to a dress showed her willingness to follow through. There was no immediate response, but he decided to wait a few more moments.

His breath left in a slow whoosh when she placed her hand in his. He'd held her hand earlier when he'd told her about what had happened the night before, but now it was all about her. A current of awareness zipped up his arm. He tugged Jessalyn closer, but didn't otherwise touch her. He drew her hand up and kissed it, all the while watching her face.

Her eyes widened and she took a few short breaths, looking away. Maybe it was a good sign for them she was affected also.

"Let's go. Time is getting short."

"Wait." She hurried to the table beside the love seat and lifted the flower ring circling the candle, placing it on her head. "What do you think?"

He chuckled. "Perfect." Maybe she was getting into this. He imagined most women wanted to plan their own weddings. And to men they were in love with. The flowers were a good sign she was accepting this surprising turn of events.

She bit her lip. "Don't you want anyone there today?"

If this were an ordinary wedding, he'd want his family present. Susan would likely be hurt she hadn't been included. Being a policeman, Gary was the last person Theo could invite to this forced wedding. Especially since, at any moment, Jessalyn might back out. So why had he chosen to have his dad's best friend, a judge, marry them when he could have found a justice of the peace? He'd wanted someone there who felt like family.

"My family's away for the weekend." They were at the family's beach house, and would have postponed their plans if he'd asked. He'd originally planned to join them, but that morning had told them, without explanation, he couldn't go.

Bradley had teased him for months about not asking Jessalyn out yet, and would be skeptical about the sudden wedding. He hoped his brother didn't cause her problems.

"Let's get going." Still holding her hand, he headed to the garage by way of the kitchen. He hoped this life-altering decision wouldn't destroy them both.

Chapter 3

Jessalyn stared at the formal white colonial home where Theo stopped. She thought they'd meet in the judge's chambers. "Where are we?"

"Judge Alvarez's house."

"His *house*? Why?" That seemed scarier than the judge's chambers. The chambers were impersonal, a man who didn't know them. Marrying at the judge's house meant the judge knew Theo, and he would particularly scrutinize her.

Theo twisted in his seat to face her, placing a hand on her arm. "He was my dad's best friend. His wife and son will be our witnesses."

She stared at her laced fingers, one with the sparkling, new diamond ring. None of her wedding daydreams featured diamonds as large as these—a round center stone with a pear-shape diamond on each side.

He rubbed her arm until she looked at him. "Please don't tell them about this deal between us. I could end up in jail. It could be construed I bought you, but I'm only trying to protect you."

Construed—it was the truth, but his face was so sincere and trustworthy. In all the months he'd come to the restaurant, she'd never gotten a bad vibe from him. He'd turned her world upside down, but had done the same to his own. Despite this crazy day, she felt safe with him.

Before arriving at Theo's house that morning, she hadn't

realized he was rich. Besides the money he'd already paid out, he was taking another chance with his wealth. "Maybe we should have a prenuptial agreement. I don't want anything more from you than what you've already paid on Mitch's behalf."

He gave her a small smile. "Those words tell me that if this doesn't work out, you wouldn't try to take every dime I have."

She wrapped her hand around his. "You've already paid out more than I've ever earned. I'm beholden to you for Mitch."

He frowned. "He drop-kicked you into what may have been a tortured death so he could walk away unscathed. This was not *your* debt to repay."

Theo sounded as angry at her brother as she felt. He hadn't stepped in to take advantage, but to protect her.

He glanced at his watch. "We've got to get inside." He held the car door open, taking her hand, then they strode up to the door. It opened moments after he rang the bell.

Jessalyn drew in a long breath to calm her nerves, preparing to face Theo's friends. He'd probably saved her life, or at least kept her from being tortured. She'd try her best to protect him from the wrong kind of scrutiny. They'd have to discuss the rest of the terms later.

An older woman stood in the doorway, smiling and enveloped Theo in a hug. "Theo, it's good to see you. I was so excited when Dom told me he'd be performing your marriage ceremony." She stepped back and took Jessalyn's hands. "And this must be Jessalyn. I'm Kelly."

"Hi." Jessalyn had no idea how to act.

"Come on through," Kelly said. "We're having the wedding in the backyard."

Theo grasped Jessalyn's hand and followed Kelly through the entry and into the living room.

At the stairs, Kelly called up. "Dom, they're here." They

continued out French doors into a flower-filled yard.

Jessalyn scanned the lawn and garden. One of the people in the household was a gardener or they hired someone. There were abundant flowers of every color. An arbor, covered in flowering vines, led deeper into the yard. "Wow. This is beautiful." She couldn't have picked a more perfect place to get married. If only everything else about the wedding could be perfect.

"Theo!" a voice behind them said.

Theo dropped her hand, spinning around. "Alex." The men hugged, pounding each others' backs.

Alex stepped back. He was about Theo's age with dark hair and the bluest eyes. Maybe they'd gone to school together. "Where's your family?"

"It's just Jessalyn and me."

Alex's eyebrows rose, and he looked her up and down, but he didn't say anything. Fortunately, because she didn't want to respond to anything he might say after that appraisal.

Theo had chosen not to have his family present, but asked a family friend to marry them. Of course, the judge wouldn't know they'd never had a single date. Maybe Theo needed some sense of family present for his wedding.

An older man, who resembled Alex, stepped outside. He strode forward, extending his hand. "Congratulations, Theo. Why the rush?"

Theo stared at Jessalyn, and if she didn't know better, she'd believe he had feelings for her. That twinkle in his eye and the parted lips, made her think he wanted to kiss her. "We wanted to elope, but between Jessalyn's schooling and my work, we don't have time to actually get away." He turned to Dom. "You're the next best thing. Do you mind?"

If he could lie so believably to a judge, she might have trouble detecting if he lied to her face. And she had to do the same thing with his family. This was no way to start a marriage.

Dom smiled. "Not at all. I'm happy you included us in your special day." He gestured to an arbor. "Let's stand there."

Theo and Jessalyn stood in front of Dom under the arbor. Alex snapped a few photos with his cell phone. If she'd been unconcerned about what it would do to Theo, she would have told Alex not to bother, but she'd promised Theo to keep it a secret.

Dom opened a book and cleared his throat. "Let's begin. Please face each other and hold hands."

Theo gazed into her eyes and grasped her much colder hands. His eyes were reassuring—exactly what she needed. A lot of women probably got really nervous at their wedding, wondering if they were doing the right thing, but it couldn't have been worse than how she felt. They weren't a real couple.

"Theo, do you take Jessalyn to be your lawful wedded wife? Do you promise to love, cherish, and respect her, in sickness and in health, for richer, for poorer, for better, for worse, and forsaking all others, keep yourself only unto her, for so long as you both shall live?"

"I do."

Their marriage would begin with a lie. They didn't know each other enough to be in love. Theo was giving up his way of life and risking his wealth for a near stranger. She had no choice, but he did, and he'd chosen to do this for her. In all ways that were important, her life *did* belong to him. She was as crazy as him for going through with this.

"...for so long as you both shall live?"

The question jolted her back to the ceremony. "I do." She hoped it was believable. She concentrated on Dom's next words.

"Do you together promise in the presence of these witnesses that you will at all times and in all circumstances, conduct yourselves toward one another as becomes husband and wife? Respond with 'we do'."

"We do."

Dom closed his book. "I now pronounce you husband and

wife." He nodded to Theo. "You may kiss your bride."

Jessalyn wished they'd practiced this ahead of time. First kiss at their wedding. She expected a quick peck, but Theo placed a hand behind her neck and leaned in. The sparkle in his eyes told her he planned on enjoying this part of the ceremony. She closed her eyes before his lips touched hers.

An awareness of him flooded her. Barely any part of them touched, but she could sense his need. She gripped his lapels—maybe to keep from falling or maybe to hold him closer. The kiss hadn't progressed to a deeper one, but it still made her light headed, causing her heart to pound.

A throat cleared beside them, and Theo stepped back. He grinned then swooped back in for the kind of kiss she'd expected the first time. A quick peck, as if he was too affected to keep his lips off her. It was exactly how she felt. If no one was around, she would have continued kissing him. That surprised her since she'd never had such a strong urge with anyone else before.

Dom climbed the stairs to the large deck and set a paper on a glass-top table. "I need signatures on the license." They all signed and Dom tucked the paper into an envelope then stuck it in his pocket. "I'll file this on Monday. Come on inside. Kelly prepared lunch."

"You didn't have to go to that trouble," Theo said. He held Jessalyn's hand, and she wondered if it was for show.

Kelly stood in the doorway. "No trouble. I just added a little extra."

Jessalyn wished they could leave instead of continuing to act like a couple in love. It was official. They were tied together by marriage, and she didn't know what to make of it.

She'd been stressed over all these changes from the moment she and Mitch had gotten home. Her initial belief she'd be a slave was equally as hard to accept as becoming a bride instead. Her head still spun at the crazy turn her life had taken. She needed time alone to put it all in perspective.

~~~

Twenty minutes after they had dessert, Theo thanked Dom for the ceremony and Kelly for the meal. Jessalyn had occasionally shifted in her chair and once her hand fluttered on his leg as if uncomfortable, but on the whole she'd handled the time with his friends well. At least she could be honest when Kelly asked her where they met, not so much when Kelly asked how long they'd dated.

Theo had jumped in, staring into Jessalyn's eyes. "It seems like forever, but it's been about three months." He wished he would have asked her out three months ago. Maybe if they'd been dating, Mitch wouldn't have been put in a position to sell his sister. The marriage might still have happened today, but they would have come into it as more than acquaintances.

She'd been the most excited when talking about nursing school. She couldn't take a full load of classes because of work, but when Alex asked about how her classes were going, she'd blushed, admitting she had a 3.9 grade point average.

He stood, and everyone else followed. Jessalyn's shoulders dropped—hopefully in relief and not resignation that she'd be alone with him.

Alex shook his hand. "Congrats, Theo." He leaned closer, lowering his voice. "She's a looker and smart, too." He resumed in a normal voice. "I'll email you the pictures."

Theo had forgotten about the photos Alex had taken during the wedding, and hoped they didn't show the nervousness he'd sensed in Jessalyn. "Thanks for doing that. I didn't think about having a photographer." If any turned out, he'd have to print one for his office, and another for their sitting room, maybe even one for the living room mantel. It might be good to send one to the newspaper, too, so it might get back to Mansard Jessalyn was off limits.

After hugs were shared, Theo helped Jessalyn into the car.

"How about a walk in the park?" She was his wife now, and although he'd been surprised by his strong reaction to kissing her, he was wary of doing it again. He'd told her they wouldn't have sex yet, and he'd keep that promise. It was best if they didn't go home where they'd be alone.

They'd have to discuss what they would tell his family, and how they should act around them.

"Okay. But nothing too rugged since I'm wearing heels." She lifted her foot.

He was distracted by her slim ankles. He hoped someday soon to kiss those ankles and nibble his way up her legs. The two inch heels wouldn't be too bad as long as he kept to sidewalks. If his family wasn't at the lake house, he'd take her there, and they could stroll barefoot on the beach. Maybe after the family came home, he'd take her there for a few days—sort of a honeymoon that wasn't. They could get used to each other without anyone around.

"Hold my hand and I'll make sure you don't stumble."

For now, he chose a park with a paved path through a garden. He helped her from the car and held her hand. He liked touching her, and was glad she didn't pull away. They started down the sidewalk.

"All the flowers here are nice," she said. "But I think Dom and Kelly's garden is more beautiful."

He'd noticed the colors at their house, but his gaze had been mostly on Jessalyn.

"I have to go into work at four-thirty," she said.

He stopped and studied her. He'd forgotten about her job. Of course. He saw her on Fridays, but hadn't considered her schedule. "Maybe you should consider giving your notice and quitting."

Her mouth firmed. "I need the money."

"Not anymore. If you quit the restaurant, it will give you more time to complete your studies. Next semester, you can take more classes and finish sooner."

She crossed her arms. "I don't want any more money from you."

The last thing they needed was an argument only hours after getting married. "I haven't given you any money, but I plan on getting a credit card issued to you."

"I don't need it. I have my own money."

An argument so soon wouldn't help them to get used to each other. He'd let this go for now. The card would be available, but he wouldn't push her to quit work, at least not until it was time to register for the next semester. He held out his hand.

She glared, but took it and they started walking again. "Can you tell me where the closest bus stop is to your house?"

"Do you really think there's a bus stop anywhere near my neighborhood?"

"I don't mind a long walk. I have to get to work and school."

"I'll take you."

She tugged her hand, but he held it tighter. "I don't expect you to take the time to do that."

He didn't like that she was angry with him, but he was proud of her independence. He needed to work harder at keeping the peace. "It's not safe for you on a bus or walking home after your late shift."

"Mitch used to pick me up after work, but I took a bus on the way, and for school."

"I'll drive you the next couple of days until we can get you a car."

She tried again to pull away, raising her voice. "You're not buying me a car."

He wrapped an arm around her and turned her to face him, then lifted her chin. "I'm the CEO of a top ten company in this state. My wife is not taking a bus." He paused for a moment and grinned. "Please?"

She laughed. "You can't use your pretty face and a 'please' to win an argument."

Maybe he hadn't won yet, but her body had relaxed, giving him a chance to convince her he wanted to keep her safe.

He couldn't believe how right it sounded calling her his wife. He stared into her eyes, trying to communicate how important she was. "I went into Zentaro's last night with the intention of asking you out." He touched her cheek with the back of his fingers. "You don't deserve to have your choices taken away from you. For that, I'm sorry. But I'm not apologizing for protecting you the only way I could. And part of that protection is to give you a car so you don't have to take the bus."

"Fine. Waste your money on a car."

"You do have a driver's license, don't you?"

She tried to step back. "Of course, I do. Mitch made sure of it."

He narrowed his eyes. "Why was he the one to ensure you got a license?"

She dropped her gaze. "Because my parents died when I was fourteen."

He hadn't considered why she lived with her brother. He must have taken care of her after they died—until he decided to sell her. She and her brother had been a small family, and now she'd lost even that. He was determined to give her his family. They'd learn to love her.

They had one sad thing in common. "I lost my mom when I was fifteen and my dad when I was twenty-four. Sunday night, you'll meet his second wife, Susan. She's five years older than me."

Jessalyn's eyes widened.

He chuckled. "I know, but they really loved each other. She's married to a cop now. You kind of met my younger brother, Bradley, at Zentaro's a while ago. Then there's my half-sister, Autumn. She's ten."

"Autumn? I think I've met her. She likes pizza with lots of

olives." Jessalyn grinned.

He laughed. "That's her." He checked the time. "We better get back to the house so you can get ready for work."

Chapter 4

They'd stopped at Theo's house long enough for Jessalyn to change, then he dropped her in front of Zentaro's. Theo touched her hand. "I'll be in the waiting area at ten."

Without looking at him, she gave a quick nod and got out. Maybe her life would feel normal for the few hours she worked.

She stored her purse and sweater in her locker and checked in with her boss. Since she didn't officially start waitressing until five, she rolled silverware into linen napkins, filling a basket with them. Then she took care of a few other organizing duties.

Karen entered the kitchen and tossed her apron into the bin with the soiled napkins. "I'm glad I've got the next two days off. Todd and I are headed out as soon as I get home." Jessalyn's coworker had talked of nothing else for the past couple of weeks.

Jessalyn snatched an apron from the folded pile on a shelf, tying it around her waist. "Have fun."

Karen raised her head toward the ceiling. "Sun, sand, and Todd. What could be better?" She grinned. "And if it rains, I've still got Todd."

Jessalyn laughed, picking up a stack of menus she'd wiped down.

"Whoa! Whoa! What's that?" Karen grabbed Jessalyn's hand and Jessalyn fumbled to put the menus down before she dropped them. "You're engaged?" Her eyes widened. "No. You're married! These rings are amazing. When did this happen?"

So much for having a normal evening. "This afternoon."

Karen propped her hands on her hips. "I didn't even know you were dating anyone, and now you're married. You've been holding out."

Karen wouldn't believe it if she told her. And she couldn't say anything. "It happened so fast." Like racecar fast.

"Who is he?"

"You know Theo Argyle?"

Karen covered her mouth. "You mean your Friday regular?" She fanned her face, leaned close and stage whispered. "Don't tell Todd, but that guy is so hot." Then she slapped Jessalyn's arm with the back of her fingers. "See, I told you he was interested in you."

Karen had, and Jessalyn hadn't believed her. She'd enjoyed talking with Theo when he came in for dinner, but hadn't thought he was any more interested than any other guy. He was super nice.

Her friend glanced at Jessalyn's ring again. "But why didn't you tell any of us you two were dating?"

Jessalyn stared at her menus. "We've been keeping it quiet."

"Yeah, so quiet you two didn't act like a couple when he came in to eat."

Jessalyn forced a grin. "I guess we were successful at keeping it a secret." She hated lies.

Her boss peeked out of his office. "Jessalyn, get out on the floor." Peter was the best boss. He used gentle reminders to keep the restaurant running smoothly.

"Okay, sorry."

Karen patted her shoulder. "Oops. See you in a couple days."

Jessalyn headed out and checked on her tables, pouring water, asking if anyone needed anything.

Saturdays were busy and this was no exception. The evening flew by. The other server and the hostess, Liz and Tammy, were excited when they discovered she'd married, and were surprised she hadn't taken time off. Time off meant going on a honeymoon the she wasn't ready for.

She'd be glad when the evening was over and the questions she didn't know how to answer would end.

She wondered about mail-order brides and intimacy a hundred-fifty years ago. Did those rough guys out west immediately expect sex? She hoped the man she'd married would keep his promise to let her decide.

At the end of the night, Jessalyn worked on the next day's prep then tossed her apron in the bin. She retrieved her purse and slipped on her sweater. In the entry, she found Theo talking to Tammy.

One thing she'd always appreciated about Theo was courtesy to all the staff. Some customers treated the servers as if they were second-class citizens. She always did her best for all customers, but some made it difficult.

She stopped beside the two and Theo stepped closer. He wrapped an arm around her waist then kissed her forehead. The contact tingled. He had to pretend he was a loving husband, but for a second, she didn't want it to be pretend. She should still be angry with him for forcing her into this situation, but when he wasn't being bossy, he was fun to be with. She'd enjoyed talking with him for months. It was hard to reconcile Theo's two sides.

He stared into her eyes. "You ready to go?"

She nodded, and only remembered Tammy when Theo told her it was nice talking with her. "Bye, Tammy."

"She's walking out with us," Theo said. He kept his arm around her as they walked outside waited for Tammy to get in her car and start it, and only dropped it when he opened the passenger door for her. Mitch used to pick her up, but he'd wait in the car.

During the fifteen minute drive back to his house, they said nothing. She usually stayed up for a short time after getting home to unwind before going to bed. Tonight, she didn't think it would be possible to unwind. Not when she thought about sleeping in the same bed as Theo.

He pulled into the four-car garage and her stomach clenched. Jessalyn got out of the car before he had a chance to come around to her side. She followed him into the mudroom which led to the kitchen. They'd been alone earlier in the house when she'd rushed upstairs to change, but her thoughts were all on getting to work. Now, with his family away, all she could think about was that they were alone together. This could determine if he would keep his word.

He shut and locked the door then pushed buttons on a security panel. "Do you have a swimsuit?"

"Why?"

He smiled. "Since you've been on your feet all night, I thought sitting in the hot tub might help you relax."

"You have a hot tub?"

"And a pool. So, do you have a suit?"

The summer before, her friend, Sally, had talked her into getting a bikini. She still had her old one-piece, but it had a saggy butt and she didn't want to wear that in front of Theo. The bikini would be scary to wear, though. "Yes."

"Do you want to try it out?"

It would be nice for her feet and legs to relax in the hot water. It might even help her sleep. "Okay."

"Good. Let's get changed."

She followed him up the stairs, all the while wondering what would happen in his bedroom. Nerves fluttered in her stomach, and she wasn't sure if it was worry or anticipation that he might touch her.

Theo chuckled when he strode through the door. "Had trouble finding the right dress?"

Changing before work, she hadn't had time to pick up the clothes she'd scattered that morning. "I packed in a hurry and with anger, so I had no idea where a suitable dress was hiding."

He crossed to the dresser, extracting swim trunks. "Come out when you're ready. There are towels in the pool room, so no need to bring one."

He closed the door and she spun around. The clothes would have to be cleared off the bed before bedtime. She folded T-shirts and shorts that should go in drawers and stacked them on the dresser. Next she pushed aside Theo's clothes in the walk-in closet and hung her dresses and blouses. The rest of the clothes still in the suitcases could be taken care of in the morning.

Her suitcase held her underwear and probably hid her swimsuit as well. She opened it and sifted through the contents. The aqua suit was easy to find once it was uncovered. She stripped and put it on, then did a slow spin in front of the dresser mirror, wondering how Theo would see her. The bikini wasn't the skimpiest she'd ever seen, but she was used to wearing one-piece suits. She covered it with the matching wrap.

She glared down at her long legs. The wrap barely covered her bikini bottoms. At the time she'd purchased it, she'd figured it would only be covering her from the car to the beach, but now Theo would see her in it, followed by what was or wasn't underneath.

She sucked in a deep breath, yanking the door open.

Theo jumped out of a chair, his gaze on her legs before it traveled up to her face. "You are gorgeous." He turned away. "Come on. Let's go."

She followed him down the stairs, and through a long hallway. They entered a humid room and Jessalyn sidestepped since she couldn't see over his broad back. It was as if she'd stepped into a terrarium. The long wall parallel to the pool and the one at the end were all glass. Every few feet, a tall, healthy plant stood in a pot. The ceiling overhead was glass, allowing a view of a dark sky and stars. "Wow. Is that pool Olympic size?"

"Yes. Dad trained for the Olympics when he was in high school, but didn't quite make the cut. He still enjoyed swimming though."

She sniffed. "I don't smell chlorine."

"It's a salt water pool. We swim nearly every day, and that much chlorine exposure isn't healthy." He pointed to the corner, at an athletic club size hot tub. "Why don't you get in while I grab towels?"

That would work perfectly. She could get underwater before he saw her in her suit. Maybe that's why he suggested it. She dropped her wrap on a nearby chair and eased into the warm water, then settled into a reclining seat with her feet up. Even without the jets on, the heat felt wonderful on her achy leg muscles and feet. Too bad he could still see her through the clear water.

Theo dropped the towels on the table beside her wrap, continuing to the wall without glancing at her. He hit a button and the jets came on, hiding her body beneath the bubbles.

He sank into a seat near her head and groaned. "It's been a long day."

"That's all on you. I was an innocent bystander."

He took hold of her hand and her heart fluttered. She didn't know how he did that to her.

"You *are* innocent in all this, but you're not a bystander. You've been a part of it from the moment George Mansard uttered your name."

She stared at the far wall. "I was surprised when you didn't come in to eat on Friday."

"I was pretty shaken up over what happened." He squeezed her hand a little too hard and she flexed her fingers. "Sorry." He loosened his grip. "Of all the nights for that to happen. I was going to ask you to go out with me."

She vaguely remembered him saying something like that

earlier, but they'd been in a heated discussion, and she hadn't wanted to be sidetracked. "Why?"

His eyebrows rose. "Because you're beautiful and I've enjoyed talking with you. You're the reason I've spent every Friday dining at Zentaro's." He kissed her hand.

She'd thought her crush on the slightly older man was one-sided, but he'd felt something, too.

She wondered how he would have asked her. "I would have said yes."

He touched her chin, turning her head to face him, then smiled. "So, how was our first date? We had a meal and a stroll in the park."

A wedding meal with people she didn't know, but she had enjoyed the time with them. They'd made her feel at ease. She smiled. "And a kiss." And vows.

He knelt beside her, giving her a tender kiss. "How about another date tomorrow?"

The wedding kiss had been hotter, but this one was sweet. "Okay," she whispered.

"Can you ride a horse?"

She sat up. "Seriously? I've been on a couple of trail rides where one horse follows the one in front of it. I'm pretty sure the horses knew more about riding than I did. But I would love to go."

"I've got a friend who owns a ranch. I'll set it up with him."

The timer turned off the jets and his gaze traveled down her body. He sucked in a breath and climbed out of the hot tub. He grabbed a towel with his back to her. "I'll shower down here. Why don't you go on up and get ready for bed?" He strode past the pool and through a door beside the towel shelves.

It happened so fast, Jessalyn didn't know what to think of his reaction, and the next time she saw him, they'd be in his room.

Chapter 5

Theo stood under the cold spray in the shower. If he hadn't left the hot tub when he did, he would have wanted to break his promise of no sex yet—on the very first day. Her bikini covered the essentials, but it still accentuated her sexy body, and had been almost too much to resist. Now, there were hours of fantasy material that would entail tugging the knots free on her top and slipping the bottoms down her long legs before enjoying every inch of her.

He groaned and stuck his face under the water. Once he was sufficiently shivering, he toweled off and wrapped it around his hips. Normally, he wouldn't walk through the house in only a towel, but the family was away. He crept into his room. The bathroom door was closed, so he strode to the dresser and found boxer briefs. He turned his back to the bathroom door in case Jessalyn came out, and slipped the underwear on. He'd love to play dirty, and not wear a T-shirt. He wasn't bodybuilder big, but he had a decent physique from swimming laps and twice a week lifting weights. For tonight, he'd give her a measure of comfort and pulled on a shirt.

Jessalyn's T-shirts and shorts were stacked in piles on the dresser. He opened the suitcases and found underwear and socks. He crowded his own underwear into his sock drawer and transferred hers into the now empty drawer. He noted the sizes with plans on buying nicer ones at a lingerie shop. He moved onto the next two drawers, placing clothes from atop the dresser into the second vacated space. He checked the closet, finding her garments hanging next to his. She had a pitifully small number of clothes. He'd have to do something about that, although it would take a lot of convincing.

He tucked her suitcases into the closet as the bathroom door opened. She wore thin cotton sleep shorts and a tank top. He had to stop staring, or he'd require another cold shower.

Jessalyn's gaze darted to the bed and dresser then back to him, snagging on his chest before meeting his eyes. He hoped that meant she liked what she saw, because he sure did.

"Where are my clothes?"

He pointed to the two drawers. "I put them away."

She bit her lip. "Where am I sleeping?"

He waved toward the bed. "In my bed."

Her eyes widened. "Where are you sleeping?"

"In my bed."

She stared at her hands, lacing them and pulling them apart to lace them again. "You've got lots of bedrooms. Why do you want me to sleep in here if we're not going to…"

"Have sex?"

She gave a quick nod without looking at him.

He'd step closer if he didn't think it would scare her. "My family would know this isn't a real marriage if we had separate rooms. And I want that someday." He didn't dare say that he thought it would happen sooner if they were within touching distance. But it wasn't only about sex. He wanted to prove she could trust him. He wanted to wake up beside her in the morning, something he'd never wanted with any other woman.

"I…ah…haven't done this before."

He took a step closer. "Haven't done what?"

She glanced at the bed again. "Slept with a man."

He let out a long breath. "Some of this is new for me, too." He wouldn't tell her he'd never slept with a woman without sex. His previous relationships had been shallow.

Red crept up her neck into her face.

He hated that he was making her so nervous. "Have you been with a man before?" He didn't expect her to be a virgin, but it would be best to know if he had to be extra careful.

She glanced down at his chest, then her gaze darted to the bed and bounced to the window. "Yes. With a high school boyfriend. We, um, never got around to doing it in a bed."

"How old are you?"

Right now, she seemed so much younger than she had earlier. "Twenty-two."

"So it's been at least four years?"

She gave a quick nod. "We broke up when he left for college. How old are you?"

"Twenty-nine. Are you okay with that?" A little late to ask.

She shrugged. "You don't look that old."

Which made him feel *really* old.

She must have seen something in his expression. "I'm okay with it."

He had no idea if her answer was for his age, wanting a real marriage someday, or sleeping beside him. He wouldn't ask because it could also mean again he'd given her no choice.

He rubbed the back of his neck. "If we're riding horses tomorrow, we should get some sleep." He hoped close proximity might draw them together faster, but what did he know?

He got into bed on the side closest to the door.

She took a couple of steps forward, her gaze focused on him, as if he might suddenly attack her.

He waved his hand over the bed. "It's a big bed."

If she slept near the edge, they'd have a couple feet of empty space between them. He wished they were as comfortable together as they'd been when they talked about horses. She'd let him kiss her, and he wished he could give her a goodnight kiss.

Jessalyn slipped into bed with her back to him. "Good-

38

night, Theo."

"Goodnight, Jessalyn." He hoped he could sleep.

~~~

Jessalyn woke but didn't open her eyes. It was nice to relax for a few more minutes, and the bed felt so much more comfortable than usual. She stretched her arm out to drape it over the edge and ran into warm, hard flesh.

Her eyes flew open, but when she tried to draw her arm back, a hand held it to those hard abs. Theo's shirt had ridden up and now her hand was splayed over his gorgeous ripples. She stilled, and stared into his eyes. Whenever this man touched her, a zap of energy flowed between them. She'd never experienced it before him. Warmth flooded her body, the kind that made her want to get closer to him.

"Morning, Jessalyn." He lifted her hand to his lips and kissed her fingers, and returned it to a clothed part of his body—over his heart this time.

The steady beat was faster than she expected. And hers sped up to match. "G'morning, Theo."

She didn't know if the intimate setting was having an effect on her or if it was the man. She'd crushed on him for months, and now she was in the same bed with him. She bit the side of her lip.

He rubbed his fingers over her hand. "I like your hand on me."

She slowly dragged it away and tucked her fist into her own chest, her gaze remaining on his serious face. She was married to this man, and her attraction for him grew every time he touched her.

He startled her with a kiss on her forehead. "Go get dressed. I'll call my friend and make breakfast."

Theo got out of bed. She couldn't keep her gaze off his sleek muscles as he pulled his T-shirt down. It was a shame he covered the tight butt of his boxer-briefs with looser sweats. He must swim a couple of miles a day.

"Do you swim a lot?"

"Every morning."

"But not this morning."

"It was more fun watching you sleep." He grinned and left the room.

It should feel creepy having someone watch her while she slept, but instead, she kind of liked that he'd enjoyed looking at her.

Jessalyn hurried through dressing in jeans and a T-shirt, then she was afraid to face him. Theo could have done anything to her while she slept and he hadn't. Seeing him in the kitchen shouldn't bother her. She dawdled, peeking into rooms with open doors. Theo's room was one of three with a sitting room attached, but his was the largest. All were bigger than the apartment she shared with Mitch, and the furnishings were expensive and beautiful. The most comfortable looking room was the family room near the front door. Mounted on the wall was a screen bigger than any she'd seen in an electronics store. Her parents had had nice furniture—nothing like this, but it was good quality. She and Mitch ended up selling most of it when they sold the house, and what they kept was now old and worn.

There was a bookcase on the far wall she wanted to check out. She was barely into the room when Theo's voice startled her, and she spun around.

"Are you ready for breakfast, or did you want to watch TV first?"

"I wanted to see what books you have."

"On the other side of the stairs, there's an office with a library's worth of books. Come on. Let's eat."

She followed him into the kitchen where the coffee aroma rivaled the best coffee shop, and the hickory scented bacon made her stomach growl. Two places were set at a table in an alcove. As she sat, Theo placed a platter of pancakes and bacon down and poured coffee for them.

"Cream or sugar?"

She shook her head. "Black." She'd started drinking coffee after her parents died, and there was never cream or sugar in the house.

Theo sat opposite her. "We're all set for riding. Alan will have horses saddled for us by ten o'clock."

"Is he riding with us?"

"No. He has other plans, so I get you to myself." He wiggled his eyebrows, and she laughed.

If he didn't attack her in bed, she wasn't worried about what would happen while they were on horses.

He cut a chunk of pancake and held it on his fork. "Jessa, how much—"

"Jessa?"

"Is it all right if I call you Jessa?"

"No one's called me that before."

"Then it'll be special for us."

His warm expression had her heart fluttering. "Okay. And I'll call you…Theo." She laughed. "Is it short for Theodore?"

The spot between his eyebrows wrinkled. "Yes. I'm named after my great-grandfather."

His full name had likely been on their marriage license, but she'd only seen the line Judge Alvarez had pointed to for her to sign. She wondered if he didn't like his full name or if there was something he didn't like about his great-grandfather.

She popped the last bite of bacon into her mouth. "Why don't I clean up the kitchen while you get dressed?"

He put his hand behind her neck and kissed her forehead then strode from the room. Maybe he was trying to make her comfortable with his touch, or maybe he really meant it. She was almost afraid to admit to herself that she kind of liked it.

~~~

Theo handed Jessa a water bottle with a strap attached, then tied the rolled blanket behind the saddle and hung the soft cooler and his water on his saddle. They stood in the shadow of the barn, and horses nickered in the attached paddock.

"Let me help you up." As she stuck her foot in the stirrup, he held her steady and lifted her into the saddle. He left his hand on her thigh, not wanting to let her go yet. "I should have thought to get you a hat."

Jessa tipped her sunglasses down and peered over the top. "These are fine."

He ran his hand down her jean-clad thigh to her knee before backing away. They'd never start their ride if he didn't stop touching her. He hoped close contact with her every chance he got would make her more comfortable with him, but it also made him want her more.

He reminded himself that he needed to think of this as their second date. Not that it was a hard and fast rule, but he tried to have a handful of dates with a woman before thinking about having sex. Jessa deserved to have time for them to get to know each other. He enjoyed spending time with her, more than any other woman he'd dated.

He mounted his horse, gave her a few instructions, then led her through a gap in the fence. They skirted an open field, where he caught a flowery scent every so often, then headed for a wide path in the woods that would take them to a view of the valley.

"I want to introduce you to my family."

She wound the reins around her hand. "When will they be home?"

"Probably around seven."

Her shoulders dropped. "Oh. I go into work at four-thirty, but I finish at nine on Sundays."

He'd forgotten about her work. Hopefully, he could convince her to quit soon. He wanted to spend evenings with her.

"I suppose I need your work and school schedules."

"I work at Zentaro's Wednesday through Sunday, starting at four-thirty, and finish at ten, except for Sundays."

He'd have her to himself only on Monday and Tuesday evenings. And not even that, really, since some of that time would be spent with his family. "And school?"

"I have classes Monday, Tuesday, and Thursday."

He wouldn't be able to take long weekends with her, unless he could convince her to take time off work, but likely that wouldn't happen often. He couldn't expect her to immediately change her life when she'd been forced into this situation. He didn't want her to feel she still had no choices. "Times?"

"Nine each morning until two."

Maybe for the next few weeks, he could leave work at two on Mondays and Tuesdays so they could spend time together. "When does the semester finish?"

"I've got six weeks left."

He wouldn't mention it yet, but when the semester ended, it would be a great time for a honeymoon. Hopefully, by then, they'd be making love.

"I have no right to ask, but I'd like to give the appearance of being happily married. My brother should still be up when we come home." He grinned. "We can practice on him."

Her brows rose. "You don't expect me to give you passionate kisses in front of your family, do you?"

"No. But don't flinch if I wrap an arm around you or hold your hand."

"I can do that."

She'd only flinched a couple of times when he'd taken her by surprise.

It wouldn't be easy convincing his family that they were in love. They knew he hadn't dated anyone seriously in months. At the very least, he didn't want them to know he'd trapped Jessa into marriage. He ran a hand down his face. It was hard enough to believe it himself.

The trail narrowed enough that they couldn't ride side-by-side. Tall grasses beside the trail had given way to dead leaves with tree branches meeting overhead like a tunnel. Theo kept checking behind to make sure Jessa was handling the incline okay. She seemed to enjoy the challenge. The path leveled out then opened into a wide expanse. He dismounted, and she stopped beside him. He helped her down then tied the horses to a tree.

After gathering the blanket and cooler, Theo took Jessa's hand and led her to a grassy area near the summit.

Jessa stared out over the valley. "Wow. I can't believe the view."

Below, the well spaced houses of the suburbs crisscrossed the landscape and cliff swallows dove into their nests. He pointed to a partial view of a body of water. "Our lake house is on that lake."

"Too bad we can't see it from here."

"We'll get there eventually." He spread the blanket and opened the cooler, removing the food and drinks he'd picked up on the way to the ranch. "Come sit down."

She flopped down beside him. "Have you been up here before?"

"Many times. But it's the first time I've been up here alone with a beautiful woman." He wanted to make it clear that this date was more important than all the others.

"Bah. You don't have to do that, you know."

He squinted. "Do what?"

"Tell me I'm beautiful. Act like you've got to win me over. You already have me."

He tipped her sunglasses down to see her eyes. "You *are* beautiful. And I don't have the most important part of you. That's what I want."

Her eyes widened. Maybe he'd said too much, too soon. He'd never courted a woman before. He'd had girlfriends, but the relationships had come about naturally and his heart hadn't been involved. Nothing like how he already felt for Jessa.

"Let's eat." He handed her a soda and set a wrapped sub sandwich in front of her.

She tore into the wrapper. "So what does a CEO do?"

"I oversee everything. All the department heads report to me. I keep an eye on future development and delegate as needed." He gave more details, and by the time he'd explained it, they'd finished eating.

Jessa lay on her side with her head propped up. "Sounds like you really enjoy it."

"Most of the time. But there's a lot of stress. A lot of people depend on me to stay ahead of any issues so we don't have to cut jobs."

"What did you do before you were CEO?"

He ran a hand through his hair. "It seems so long ago. I became CEO when my father died five years ago. I was VP of Engineering. I was involved in the projects that keep this company on the cutting edge. Every stage from brainstorming to concept to pre-production." He gave her some anecdotes from his early days.

"It sounds like you enjoyed engineering more than being CEO."

"I..." He hadn't spent time thinking about it. It was expected that he step into the CEO position when his father died. "You know? You're right. I do what has to be done, but I enjoyed my job more when I was head of engineering."

"Why don't you take over engineering again and promote Bradley to CEO?"

He widened his eyes. "That's brilliant and worth thinking about. Maybe I'll ask Bradley what he thinks. He's three years older now than I was when I took over, and I'd be there as a sounding board."

He lay on his side next to her and kissed her. He'd have to make a conscious effort to not take this too far. He wanted to do so much more, but this was unofficially their second date. With his wife—which made it that much harder to resist. He'd never had to think about holding off, but it had never felt this right so early in a relationship.

He ran a finger down the side of her face. "You are so special. More than—"

She sat up, wrapped her arms around her up-drawn legs, and stared out over the valley. "I should be doing homework right now."

He'd overstepped. It would probably embarrass her if he apologized. She'd likely say he had every right to touch her, but touching a woman wasn't a right. He wanted her to *want* him to touch her.

Her independence seemed so important to her, and he wouldn't do anything that would jeopardize her schooling. "Let's leave. You can do your homework poolside while I swim, if you want. Maybe if you finish early enough, you can join me."

They packed up and mounted their horses. It would take careful planning to make time to spend with her, but it would be worth it.

Chapter 6

Rather than eating alone at the house, Theo enjoyed an early dinner at Zentaro's. Today, he hadn't wanted to drop Jessa off and not see her for the entire evening. She stopped by and talked for a minute or two every chance she got, which was more often than before, when he was an ordinary customer. He hoped it was because she didn't want them to be parted either.

After he arrived home, he read a book in the living room for an hour before his family's voices in the kitchen alerted him they'd returned from the weekend away. He joined Susan and Autumn as Bradley and Gary came in, both with bags in their hands.

"I'll help you unload." Theo headed into the garage.

They'd taken two cars and both trunks were open. He lifted a cooler from Susan's car and carried it into the kitchen, then followed Gary out. Gary picked up the last bag from Susan's car and Theo grabbed the remaining items from Bradley's trunk, then closed it.

Inside, he set the laptop on the table as Autumn took her backpack from him. She dropped the pack and grabbed his hand. "Theo! Is that a wedding ring?"

Leave it to his little sister to notice. She probably had wedding rings on her mind since her mom had married Gary a month ago.

All talking ceased and everyone stared at him.

It wasn't the way he'd planned on telling them, but if he

wanted to do it differently, he should have removed the ring. Maybe subconsciously he wanted it discovered right away. He wiggled his fingers in the air. "Yes."

"Who?"

"When?"

"What?"

The voices chorused so that he couldn't tell who asked which question. Not that it mattered. "I got married yesterday."

Bradley punched Theo's arm. "You weren't dating anyone." He yanked Theo close and whispered in his ear. "You didn't find out you got some girl pregnant, did you?"

The air froze in Theo's lungs. It was exactly what he should have expected from his brother. "No," he said under his breath, then spoke to everyone. "I married Jessalyn Waters. We met at Zentaro's where she works."

Bradley's eyebrows rose.

Autumn jumped up and down. "I know Jessalyn. She's so nice. She gives me extra olives on my pizza."

At least his new wife had one fan in the house.

A crease marred the space between his stepmother's eyebrows. "Theo, why didn't you wait until we could all attend? Why the rush?"

"Were you drunk?" Gary asked. Leave it to the cop to ask that.

"No. We weren't drunk. Dom Alvarez wouldn't have married us if we were."

Gary wrapped an arm around his wife. "Judge Alvarez married you?"

Theo shrugged. Gary wouldn't know about the connection. "Family friends. It was sort of spur of the moment. Sorry, Susan." After all of them being present for her and Gary's wedding, he understood her disappointment. The decision had been made in the wee hours of the morning, so he wasn't really lying.

"When is she moving in?" Susan asked.

"She already has. She lived with her brother, so only her clothes had to be moved. If anyone's up, you can meet her when I get back from picking her up at work at nine-thirty. Or you can wait until morning." He hoped they'd all go to their suites for the night and put off meeting Jessalyn, but knew they wouldn't wait. He opened the cooler and transferred leftovers, snacks, and drinks to the refrigerator.

"Mom, can I stay up?" Hopefully, Autumn's excitement would rub off on the others.

Susan wrapped an arm around Autumn's shoulders. "No, honey. You can see her in the morning. Go take your bath, and I'll be up soon."

Autumn stuck out her bottom lip. "Fine. Goodnight everyone."

No one spoke until Autumn's footsteps faded up the stairs.

Theo closed the refrigerator door and turned around.

Susan crossed her arms. "What's going on, Theo? You never jump this fast into anything."

She was right. Stodgy Theo who always examined every decision from six sides. Except this one. He'd jumped into the fray with his heart, reacting on instinct to protect Jessa. "Jessa needs me, and I need to be there for her. Wait until you meet her, you'll love her." He wasn't quite ready to say *he* loved her.

Susan bumped her hip into Gary, and he settled his arm around her waist. It was as if they were teaming up on him. "Is she pregnant?"

This interrogation couldn't feel any more like he was a teenage boy being questioned by his parents about his conduct with his girlfriend. "No! Can you withhold any other judgments until after you get to know her?" Hopefully, he'd get to know her faster than they would.

Bradley narrowed his eyes then walked away. That look meant they weren't done. Too bad. He was.

Theo strode into the living room, sat down and picked up

his book. He pretended to immerse himself in the story and ignored everyone. It might have been childish, but he didn't want to defend himself when he didn't have a defense he could talk about.

~~~

Like the night before, Jessalyn found Theo waiting inside the restaurant's front door at the end of her shift. She liked it.

Theo opened the car door for her. "Autumn saw my wedding ring. Everyone but Autumn will be up to meet you when we get home."

Jessalyn wished she could sneak in and not deal with anyone until morning. The night had been busy with one server short, and she was too tired to think straight. She hated not telling the truth, but understood Theo's hesitation. He got in the driver's side and started the car.

She kicked off her shoes. "Okay. So, how are we doing this?" She'd let him figure it out since he got them into this marriage. Except she'd have to play along.

"I told them it was a spur of the moment decision and that you weren't pregnant." He glanced at her stricken face. "They asked."

He wrapped his hand around hers. "It might stop some questions if they catch us kissing when we get into the house."

Something fluttered in her stomach. If his planned kiss was anything like the one at their wedding, Theo would have to pick her up off the floor. "Would that work?"

"It might save us from telling some half-truths." He grinned. "But if it doesn't work, at least I got to kiss you."

That smoldering smile while talking about kissing almost did her in. "Okay. I'm game." Big time. She'd be a fool to turn down a kiss, but he didn't deserve her to be so agreeable.

Theo drove into his space between Susan's and Bradley's

cars in the garage, and they made their way into the kitchen. Once the door was closed, he kept his word. He pushed her back to the door, lifted her chin with a finger, and teased her with little kisses. It wasn't what she'd hoped for, but he probably thought it was enough to fool his family. She threw her arms around his neck and held his head so he couldn't pull away. He growled and deepened the kiss. Finally.

She liked the taste of him and his woodsy smell. His hard chest pressed against her breasts and the evidence of him wanting her quickened her breathing. She ran a hand through his hair.

Bradley's voice brought her back to reality. "You know you've got a bedroom upstairs."

Her face heated. She'd forgotten where they were and that this display of affection was supposed to be for show.

Theo slowed his kisses and tipped back. He quirked a brow. "You okay?"

She gave a quick nod.

He whispered in her ear. "I wish the house was still empty." He spun to greet his brother, keeping her behind him—maybe giving her a chance to recover.

She stepped to the side. "Hi, Bradley."

The man's gaze ping-ponged between them, and she wondered what he thought.

"Hi, Jessalyn. I'm kind of surprised."

"Yeah, me, too. It was all such a rush."

He narrowed his eyes. "Why the—"

"Oh, you're back," a red-headed woman entered the room, fortunately, interrupting Bradley. A man, a couple of inches taller than her, followed behind. She held out her hand and Jessalyn shook it. "I'm Susan Wassman. This is my husband, Gary."

Jessalyn had seen Susan and Gary before, but hadn't learned their names.

"Susan was married to my dad," Theo said. "Autumn's has

gone to bed already."

Susan didn't appear to be more than a couple years older than Theo. And he'd been worried about *their* age gap?

She studied the four of them. She'd have to be on her guard constantly. Or maybe not. She was a new addition to the household, and of course, everyone was curious. Hopefully, there would be privacy sometimes.

Susan took her husband's hand. "Gary, Autumn, and I live in the right wing. We're house hunting and should be gone in a couple of months." She laughed. "But we'll probably be back regularly so Autumn can use the pool."

Jessalyn glanced at Theo, then all the others. She felt like she was behind bars in a zoo with everyone waiting for her to do tricks. The night had already been too long. She stifled a yawn. "I'm sorry, but I had an exhausting night. Would you mind if we got to know each other tomorrow?"

Susan's face softened. "Of course, dear. We'll probably only see each other for a few minutes in the morning. Will you be home for dinner?"

"Yes, I'm not working tomorrow. It was nice meeting you." She glanced at Theo as he held out his hand. They took a few steps when Bradley stopped them.

"Theo, can we talk for a minute?"

Theo grimaced, and kissed Jessalyn's cheek. "I'll be up soon."

Jessalyn walked away as gracefully as she could. She didn't want anyone to think she was running from them, though in her head she was.

She collected sleep shorts and a tank top and escaped into the bathroom. After a quick shower, she got dressed. She wished she was bold enough to go down and use the hot tub. It would relax her aching feet and muscles better than the shower.

She picked up a textbook and climbed into bed. She wouldn't be able to sleep until Theo told her about the talk with

Bradley. It almost felt like they were trying an intervention with him—like she was some kind of dangerous drug.

At the end of the chapter, she'd had enough, so she placed the book on the bedside table. She'd expected Theo to be ten to fifteen minutes, but a half-hour had passed. She scooted down in bed and tucked the covers under her chin.

The sitting room door opened and closed. Theo paused in the bedroom doorway, staring at her.

Jessalyn propped herself up on her elbows. "Was it bad?"

Theo crossed the room and sat beside her. "Bradley asked if you coerced me into marrying you."

Not too surprising since she was a nobody, and not beautiful, despite Theo saying she was. "I assume you didn't tell him that you coerced me."

He ran a hand through his hair. "I told him I asked you twice before you said yes."

She sat up straight. "And why did I refuse the first time?"

He shrugged. "I didn't say why."

She bit her lip. "Do you think he'll ask me? What do I say if he does?"

He took her hand, and that little zing screamed up her arm. "You could say you didn't take me seriously the first time."

"That makes sense since you're a rich CEO, and I'm a lowly waitress."

"Hey, you're not a lowly waitress. You're a nursing student who needed to support herself. And I was interested in you before I found out you're a nursing student."

He made the marriage sound real, and as if he'd had to work at getting to know her. She was having a hard time remembering what was real and what was pretend, and it'd only been a day-and-a-half.

"Okay, that's what I'll say. What else did you two talk about?"

"He doesn't buy that we were dating secretly since he and I drive to and from work together most days. Pretty much the only time we could have dated was the nights I ate at Zentaro's. And he wondered why we would have dated secretly. He asked if I was ashamed of you." Theo blew out a long breath. "I really didn't think this through."

A surprising pain twisted in her chest. "If you had, you wouldn't have married me?"

His eyes widened. "What? No. I still would have. I should have thought out the details more. Like maybe waiting a couple of weeks to get married with family present." He stood. "You should get some sleep. There's one more family member to meet. At least Autumn is excited about it, but she'll probably have a million questions."

She was sure she'd have nightmares. "Goodnight." She lay down as Theo headed into the bathroom. While Autumn was asking her a million questions, the rest of the family would likely be listening with rapt attention to every response she gave. That seemed scarier than what she'd gone through so far.

Chapter 7

Jessalyn woke alone in the center of the bed. She hoped she'd scooted over after Theo got up. She rushed getting dressed, stuffed her books into her backpack, and crept downstairs. In this big house, she felt more like an interloper now that Theo's family was home. Voices talked over each other in the kitchen but as soon as she entered, they stopped and all eyes were on her.

Hopefully it didn't remain like this for long. Of course, Gary was an outsider a short time ago, but seemed to be part of the family now. He must have had some dealings with the family before marrying Susan which would have made a huge difference in being accepted. Jessalyn was a stranger who barely knew her husband, and these people didn't know her at all. If she was a less brave woman, she'd run back to her room and wait for them to leave, but it would be easier to handle this now than later.

Theo was nowhere in sight. It would have been nice to have his support this morning.

"Good morning, everybody."

Autumn got up from the table and hugged Jessalyn. "You're my sister now."

Jessalyn grinned. "I guess I am. I've always wanted a sister." Which was true.

Susan glanced at the wall where there was a clock. "Autumn, you have to finish your breakfast so we can leave for

55

school."

"Okay, Mom." She tugged Jessalyn's hand. "Can you sit beside me?"

"Ah, sure."

Susan pointed to a warming tray on the counter. "Jessalyn, there's pancakes, sausage, and eggs."

"Thanks. Do you always have such a big breakfast?" She didn't want these people to feel she was taking advantage of them.

"Miriam makes breakfast every morning she's here."

"Who's Miriam?" Theo hadn't mentioned her name.

"She's our cook-slash-housekeeper. We'd be lost without her. She refuses to eat breakfast with us, so we'll have to introduce you later."

Jessalyn loaded her plate with food. Normally, she grabbed an apple or made some toast with peanut butter. She sat down beside Autumn, and poured syrup on her pancakes. Her first bite was heaven—real maple syrup, and light, fluffy pancakes that didn't come from a box. There might have been a hint of vanilla.

"Are you still going to work at Zentaro's?" Autumn asked. "I like when you're there."

"That's my plan." Jessalyn surprised herself by not sounding as determined as she should have. Maybe Theo was influencing her. She didn't want that. If he decided to end this game, she'd need to take care of herself. She still had a year-and-a-half of school left at the pace she was going.

A hand gripped her shoulder, making her jump. She hoped no one noticed.

"Morning, baby." Theo kissed the top of her head. "You were still asleep when I went down for my swim."

She supposed he had to give everybody the illusion that they were sleeping together like husband and wife. Her face probably wouldn't be flaming like this if they were doing all that husband-wife stuff.

He sauntered to the warming tray and picked up a sausage link with his fingers, eating it in two bites then poured a cup of coffee. He placed two more links on a plate and joined them at the table. "Morning, all."

He didn't seem to mind the way everyone watched the two of them. Theo sipped his coffee. "Bradley, we'll have to drive separately. I'm dropping Jessa at school."

Bradley raised his brows. "I don't mind making a detour to the college."

"I'm leaving work early and picking up Jessalyn after class to take her car shopping. We won 't be stopping back home before."

Three sets of eyes seemed to accuse her of being a gold digger. Jessalyn ran her gaze over the family. No one said anything. "It wasn't my idea. I wanted to find the nearest bus stop."

"Why do you want to ride a bus instead of drive a car?" Autumn asked.

She didn't want to have this discussion. "Because I'm used to taking the bus, and it's cheaper."

"And I think driving is safer," Theo said.

Bradley snickered. "First fight?"

Jessalyn grinned. They'd been married not quite two full days and had already argued about money, her job, a car, and…getting married. "You can tell who won. Of course, I don't have a car yet."

Susan stood up. "Jessalyn, I wish we had more time to talk, but we have to leave. Autumn, get your backpack."

In short order everyone gave their goodbyes and cleared out except Jessalyn and Theo.

Theo rested his arm on the back of Jessalyn's chair. "What time do you want to be at school?"

"Ten before nine so I have time to get to class."

"We'll leave at eight-thirty."

Ten minutes that they'd be home alone together, then the drive to school. Despite the hours together over the past two days, she was on edge. "I'm going to brush my teeth."

She didn't know how she'd shared a bed for two nights with this man and still felt a little uncomfortable with him so near. He'd been a perfect gentleman, and she hoped it continued.

~~~

Promptly at two-fifteen, Theo waited in his car in the same spot he'd dropped Jessa off. He tipped his head against the headrest and closed his eyes, reliving waking that morning, like he had a hundred times that day.

Jessa's warm body had been pressed against his chest, her head under his chin, and her top leg between his. Each had an arm wrapped around the other. He'd been hard against her belly.

His first instinct was to wake her with kisses, and overwhelm her senses. It took every honorable bone in his body to extricate himself without waking her. He'd grabbed his swim trunks and robe, fleeing to the pool. It had taken many laps before his body had cooled enough to join everyone.

The passenger door opened, and Jessa climbed in. "It's kind of nice not taking the bus home, although there's a bus stop over there." She pointed to where a few students stood next to a bus stop sign.

Theo was glad she now saw the benefit of owning a car, so he didn't feel as if he was pushing her. Or maybe she'd resigned herself to giving in and was looking at the bright side.

He faced her. "We haven't decided on what kind of car to get you." He patted the top of the seat behind her head. "Do you want one like this?"

She laughed. "A high-end Lexus is kind of pretentious for

me."

He lifted a brow, wondering if that's how she saw him.

She touched his arm. "But it suits you. You need the successful image."

He held back a chuckle at the way she tried to unruffle his feathers. "What do you want?"

She shrugged. "We could get a used car."

He shook his head. "I'm not taking a chance on unreliable transportation." He'd never met a woman so against receiving gifts. Other women he dated took the jewelry he gave them and fawned over it, but didn't seem to appreciate the thought he put into it. "If you close your eyes and imagine driving a car, what do you see?"

He was surprised when she did close her eyes, and relaxed back into the seat.

A slow grin spread across her face. "A red Mustang convertible."

He hadn't taken her for a sports car fan. "Stick shift?"

She wrinkled her nose. "Oh. I don't know how to use one."

"I'll teach you. If you're getting a sports car, it's more fun with manual shift."

"I think my dad's had that."

"Your father owned a Mustang?"

"A red convertible. He was driving it when…" She stared at the clenched hands in her lap. "—when a teenager, joyriding in a pickup, ran a red light."

He covered her hands with one of his. She'd lost both her parents in that accident. "Are you sure you want the same kind of car?"

She looked him in the eyes. "Yes. I have a lot of good memories of Dad taking us out for drives. We'd stop at a park or a picnic table by a river, and Mom served us sandwiches and chips for lunch."

"It sounds nice." He faced forward and started the car.

"Let's go test drive some Mustangs." The dealership his family bought their Lexuses also sold Fords.

It was a short drive from the college to the sprawling car lot on the edge of town. Theo parked near the door and before they reached it, his usual salesman bustled out.

Andrew shook Theo's hand. "Mr. Argyle, are you trading in your LS already?"

Theo had only owned it a year and usually held onto his cars for three. He wrapped an arm around Jessa's waist. "No. I'm buying a car for my wife."

"An LS like yours?"

"No. She wants a Mustang."

"I don't have the high-end model at this location, but I can get it in a couple days."

Theo glanced at Jessa. She'd throw a fit if he bought her the most expensive one. "Let's see what you have."

Andrew gestured to a golf cart. "Climb in. I'll take you to our stock."

Theo helped Jessa into the backseat. After she slid over, he climbed in beside her. The cart took off with a jerk, and drove along the front of the lot. At the end, Andrew hung a right and stopped. They all got out, and Andrew gestured toward several cars. "There you are. Have a look around."

Jessa circled the closest red one.

Theo stood back and spoke to Andrew. "We'll test drive an automatic and a stick, but I want to buy a stick."

"We can do that." The man raised his voice. "Mrs. Argyle, the doors are unlocked, so you can sit inside them. Once you make a selection, I'll get keys for a test drive." He leaned against the golf cart.

Jessa's eyes widened, and he wondered if it was because this was the first time she'd been called Mrs. Argyle. He liked the way it sounded, but wasn't sure if she did. She opened the door and sat inside, wiggling around, adjusting the mirror and holding the steering wheel. She went to the car parked beside it, but didn't get past the sticker—must be a more expensive model. His wife was frugal, but she'd had to be after her parents died. She moved onto the next and sat inside.

He sauntered to the first car and scanned the sticker, then headed to the one she'd bypassed. Yeah, the GT model was significantly more.

After she'd checked out all the Mustangs, she joined him, and whispered. "I'm sure they have some nice used Mustangs in their lot."

He whispered back. "We're buying new. Which do you like best?"

She stared at him for several seconds. Her shoulders dropped and she pointed to the first car she'd checked out. "That one."

It wasn't the cheapest car, but it was far from the most expensive. "Is it a stick?"

She shrugged.

He checked and found it was. Perfect. He peeked into the other models until he found an automatic, then strode back to Andrew. "We'll test drive that one and that one." He pointed to the two.

Andrew wrote the numbers on a pad of paper. "I'll be back in a couple minutes."

Five minutes later, Andrew returned. "Mr. Argyle, we've got your license on file still. Which car first?"

"The blue one," Theo said. He took the key and held it out to Jessa. "Here, baby."

She leaned close. "I'm afraid to drive it out of here. All these cars are so expensive."

"All right. I'll drive it to a side street."

Andrew headed toward the car and snapped on the dealer plate.

Theo held up his hand. "We're test driving alone."

"Yes, Mr. Argyle. I'll drive the other car to the office and you can exchange them there."

They got in the car, and Theo found a quiet street where they exchanged places. Jessa's knuckles turned white as she gripped the steering wheel.

He touched her hand. "Hey, when's the last time you drove?"

"Two weeks ago, but Mitch's car is fourteen years old, and this one is new and expensive."

He massaged her shoulder. It'd be the cheapest car he ever bought. "Relax. Take a breath." He waited for her shoulders to drop. "Okay. Give it a try."

The longer she drove, the more confident she became.

"Let's return to the dealership and try the other car," Theo said. "What do you think of this one?"

"It's nice."

He grinned. "Ask a teenage boy what he thought about driving a new Mustang, and he'd be whooping it up."

She approached the spot where they'd changed places earlier. "Do you want to take over?"

"You seem more comfortable now. Why don't you drive it in?"

She made a rueful expression. "Then I'd have to park it."

"Okay, pull over."

In minutes, Theo parked in front of the office.

Andrew stepped outside. "How was it?" He probably hoped they'd take this one since it was a more expensive car.

"Good. We're ready to try the other one." Theo traded keys with the man. "We'll meet you inside when we're done."

Once Theo was on the side street, he stopped.

Jessa leaned away from him. "I'm not driving this one."

He chuckled. "I was only going to give you some instructions." He explained the basics as he put the car through the gears. Then he headed for the curvy roads he usually test drove on. He probably shouldn't, but he pulled over and put the top down. After, he flew through the gears, getting up to speed, and took the turns faster than he would with his own car. The Mustang handled beautifully. Maybe he should have bought himself a second car long ago for weekend drives.

He glanced at Jessalyn's wide smile, happy that he'd been able to please her. Too bad they couldn't take the car out longer. They'd have to do it again after their purchase, maybe packing a lunch as her family had. A few minutes later, he turned around in the middle of a quiet intersection and drove the winding lanes back to the car lot.

As he turned into the dealer's lot, Jessa said, "That was fun."

Theo pulled into the space beside his car, turning to her. It was nice she'd enjoyed their car. "Okay. Now the big decision. Do you want this car with the stick shift, or do you want another the same color with automatic transmission?"

"How long do you think it will take to teach me?"

He shrugged. "I learned in a few hours. Some people take longer." He tapped the top of the gearshift. "One advantage of this is that fewer people can steal them since they don't know how to drive stick."

She laughed. "Seriously?" He loved to see her happy.

"Well, it's not a deterrent against a professional thief, but a joyriding kid? Definitely. So, which do you want?"

Her gaze darted between the two cars. "This one." She patted the console.

"Okay. Let's go sign the paperwork."

They entered the building and found Andrew leaning against a high counter, talking to a woman.

Theo pointed a thumb over his shoulder. "We'll take the second one."

Andrew straightened up. "Good. Good. Let's go take care of paperwork."

Theo could imagine the man rubbing his hands together. Although the car wasn't expensive like his usual choice, it was an unexpected sale.

Andrew led them into a cubicle. "Have a seat." He picked up a pad of paper. "Let me get the VIN and mileage."

A couple of minutes later Andrew returned and sat at his computer, then typed in the information. "Will the car be owned jointly?"

"No," Theo said.

"Theo—" The man started typing.

"No. Jessalyn Argyle."

Jessa grabbed his arm. "What? It's all mine? But—"

Theo grasped her hand. "Baby, I said we were getting *you* a car. This will belong to you."

Her mouth hung open, and a sheen of tears misted her eyes. Some women would take it as their due that their husbands bought them cars. Jessa was overwhelmed by his gesture. He couldn't help it. He kissed her, taking full advantage of her open mouth. He pushed a hand into her hair. The only reason he stopped was that Andrew cleared his throat.

Theo chuckled. "Sorry." He grinned at Jessa's mortified expression.

Andrew's gaze stayed on his computer screen. "Usual address?"

"Yes. And I'll contact my insurance agent when we're finished so she can handle the registration and drop off the plates."

Andrew printed out the sales pages. "All right. We need the transfer of funds." He flipped the pages around and pointed. "This amount to this account." He touched another number on the sheet.

Theo keyed the necessary information into his phone. "All set."

Andrew checked his computer and grinned. "Now, Mrs. Argyle, if you could sign here." He pointed to lines on the two pages and handed her a pen.

Jessa looked at Theo and he gave a nod. She signed her new name, with a slight hesitation the first time.

He felt good being able to do this for her.

Andrew turned the sheets around and signed them. He stood, holding one page to Jessa. "This is your copy. Come back tomorrow afternoon to collect the car."

They shook hands and Theo led Jessa outside. She stopped beside the Mustang and peered up at him then gave him a hug. "I can't believe you bought this for me."

He hadn't seen anyone so appreciative of a gift. He gave her a long kiss, but shorter than he wanted to. "You're welcome."

Chapter 8

Jessalyn pulled into a space in the employee area of Zentaro's parking lot. She got out and stared at the shiny, red Mustang. This was her car. It would probably feel even better if she'd paid for it herself, but it felt pretty darn good to have such a gorgeous car she could call her own.

Her new parking sticker graced the upper passenger corner of the windshield. She'd left early for work and stopped by the campus to register her car. Theo had given her gear-shifting lessons after they picked up the car, and again this morning, declaring her competent. She didn't shift as smoothly as he did, but it would come with practice. She agreed with him that it was more fun driving the stick.

The lessons had made him miss even more work, but that was on him. His being so nice to her, as if their relationship hadn't begun as coercion, had her forgetting how they started. She was falling for him. It was more than a crush now, but she didn't know if he was falling for her, too, or if he was a good actor, making the best of a situation he'd forced them into.

Tammy's rusty, old car parked beside Jessalyn. She got out. "What are you doing out here?"

Jessalyn patted her car. "I just got here."

Tammy's eyes widened. "In that? Whose is it?"

"It's mine. Th—"

"Your husband bought it for you? Can you help me find

one of those?"

Jessalyn laughed. "A husband or a car?"

"A rich husband. Does he have any brothers?" She wiggled her eyebrows.

Jessalyn started walking. "He's got one, but I thought you had a boyfriend."

Tammy fell in beside her. "I do, but he'd never buy me a car like this, let alone be able to afford it." She grinned. "But I really can't complain. He's got other great qualities."

In the back room, they stored their purses and tied on aprons, then joined the other servers for the shift change.

Tammy grabbed Karen's arm. "Whoa, you two. You should see Jessalyn's new car."

Liz grinned. "Did that handsome husband of yours buy it for you?"

"Yes. A Mustang."

"Seriously?"

"Oh, yeah," Tammy said. "You should see it. It's so sweet." She touched her fingertips to her lips and threw a kiss.

Karen glanced behind her. "I'll have to check it out when I leave. See you girls later." She headed into the back room.

Jessalyn grabbed a tablet and signed in. She checked on all the tables in her section—made sure the empty ones were properly set and the customers didn't need anything. The first hour was always slow on weekdays.

By six-thirty, all Jessalyn's tables were occupied. She took orders and chatted with the regulars. A shiver skittered down her spine. She wasn't sure what made her do it, but instead of spinning around to see what might have caused it, she positioned herself at the next table in such a way to see who had been behind her. As she spoke to the customer at the head of the table, she took covert glances across the next table. A man with gray at his temples, and surprising muscles for his age, stared at her. He might have been in the restaurant before, but she couldn't remember for sure. She didn't know what it was, but bad vibes radiated around him.

She caught Liz in the kitchen. "That man at table seven, has he been acting kind of weird?"

Liz shrugged. "It feels kind of icky talking to him, but he hasn't done or said anything inappropriate. It's weird because I've had guys make passes at me or ask me out and never felt anything like that."

"Exactly," Jessalyn said. "I felt him watching me and it gave me cold shivers."

Liz leaned close. "I hope he's gone by the time we close."

"Let's make sure you, Tammy, and I leave together." Theo had insisted that she walk out with someone.

Liz nodded. "I'll give her a heads up."

For the next half-hour Jessalyn forced herself to do her job. She would have much rather hidden in the kitchen until the creepy guy left.

Finally, when she returned from one of her many trips to the kitchen with a tray of food, his table was empty. Jessalyn caught Liz on the way back to the kitchen. "What was creepy guy's name?"

Liz shook her head. "I have no idea. He paid with cash. I hope he never comes back."

At the end of the evening, after the customers were all gone and the work done, the three women headed outside.

A black car with dark windows sat on the street near the women's cars. No one had ever parked there until tonight and with creepy guy on her mind, she couldn't help but think the worst. The streetlight overhead revealed the silhouette of one man at the wheel, but the back windows were too dark to tell if there were others. "Let's all leave the lot together, and follow each other for a few blocks."

"Good idea." Tammy's voice quivered. "And lock our doors immediately."

Liz's car beeped and the lights flashed. "Let's run."

The other two beeped their locks and the three women ran the remaining twenty feet to their cars. The doors slammed one after the other, and Jessalyn hit her lock button. Her heart pounded as she jammed the key in the ignition and...it tried but wouldn't start. No! This was supposed to be a new reliable car.

She jumped out and knocked on the passenger window of Liz's car and yelled through the glass. "My car won't start."

The lock clicked, and Liz called out, "Get in. Quick."

Jessalyn dove in and the doors locked behind her. She strapped the seatbelt on. "Let's get out of here." Her breath rasped in and out as if she'd run a mile.

Liz backed out of the space and followed Tammy from the lot. Jessalyn turned to see the black car fell in behind them. A few blocks along, Tammy took a left, and the black car continued behind Jessalyn and Liz.

"Don't go to either of our houses yet. See if you can lose them."

If they'd gone out individually, she'd have been stuck alone. It couldn't be a coincidence that car stood at the curb and her brand new car wouldn't start.

~~~

Theo checked his watch for the hundredth time. Jessa should have been home a half-hour ago. He'd started calling after she was fifteen minutes late with all calls going to voicemail. At first, he thought she may have had extra work to do after closing, but now he was worried. She should have called. Her first time driving home from work, and she was late. Maybe she joined the other women for drinks after work, but finishing so late, and with school the next day, it didn't seem likely. And there was no phone call.

He yanked out his phone and called her number for the fifth time—voicemail again. He ran a hand through his hair. He was probably overreacting, but he'd been on edge most of the evening. He strode through the kitchen, and flung open the door to the garage. It would ease his mind if he got to Zentaro's and found she was still there.

He strode toward his car in the last space and was behind Bradley's Porsche when Jessa's garage door started to rise. Relief warred with anger.

Jessa stood at the keypad beside the door and another car drove into her space. This couldn't be good.

Her eyes were wide, and her whole bottom lip was tucked between her teeth. He stepped behind the strange car and Jessalyn must have seen him. She lunged into his arms. He held her tight and buried his nose into her neck. She trembled. The driver's door opened and Liz stepped out, her face as shell-shocked as Jessa's.

He stared into Jessa's eyes. "What's going on?"

Tears spilled down her cheeks.

He steered them out of the garage. "Let's go inside. It looks like both of you could use a drink." He seated them in the living room and poured glasses of scotch.

He sat beside Jessa, and her leg trembled where it touched his. He dragged her onto his lap, waiting impatiently while the women drank down some fortification. "Okay. Tell me what happened."

They took turns telling him about the man in the restaurant and the SUV on the street.

Jessa drew in a shuddering breath. "The car kept following us after Tammy turned. We didn't want him to find out where we lived, so we had to lose him."

Liz crossed her arms and rubbed her biceps. "I've never driven so crazy in my life. I thought my car might tip over on some of those fast turns. It took a while to lose him."

Jessa's grip on his arm tightened. "Once he almost rammed us, and all I could do was yell *faster*. I was sure we'd have an accident."

Liz buried her face in her hands. "I've never been so scared."

Theo tightened his arms around Jessa. He could have lost her tonight, never knowing what happened to her. "The three of you should have gone back inside and called the police."

"I didn't think of it until we were trying to get away from him," Jessa said.

Liz drew in a long breath. "It's probably safe to go home now."

"No!" Jessa's expression begged him. "We have space for her tonight, don't we?"

"Yes, of course. Liz, I'll follow you home in the morning and check out your house. It's safer if you stay here." He glanced at Jessa. "And Jessalyn will sleep better knowing you're not alone."

"Thank you." She fell back against the couch.

He nudged Jessa, and they stood. He took her hand. "This way, Liz."

Theo stopped at the second door from the top of the stairs. "The bathroom in your room has everything you'll need. We'll see you in the morning.

Jessa touched Liz's arm. "I'll bring you some pajamas."

"Thanks so much." Her door closed as they continued up the hallway.

They entered their sitting room, and he hugged Jessa. Her trembling was gone, but he could imagine she was still shook up.

She kissed his cheek. "I have to get some pajamas for Liz." She strode to her dresser and pulled out flannel pants with images of cats and a T-shirt, then left the room.

Theo removed his shirt, shoes, and socks before Jessa returned. "I'm going to hold you tonight after you get ready for bed."

She didn't protest, but gathered her pajamas and went into the bathroom. He took off his pants and got into bed. Jessa came out of the bathroom and crawled in beside him, and he drew her into his arms. The tightness in his chest began to unwind. She rested her head on his shoulder, then he kissed her temple. "The past three mornings, I woke with you in my arms like this."

She lifted her head and stared at him.

He gave her a gentle kiss on the lips. "I thought it was best to leave before you woke up."

She lowered her head again. "I didn't know."

"I didn't think we were ready for that."

She rubbed her fingers on his bare chest near his neck. "But now—"

He wrapped a hand around hers. "Right now, I think you need to be held, and I need to go to sleep knowing you're right here and safe." If she hadn't had the scare, having her in his arms like this might have pushed him to break his promise. The urge had to go away.

"I need that, too. Thank you." She kissed his chest, and he held his breath to prevent the groan that wanted to break out.

"Goodnight, Jessa."

She snuggled closer and her breast brushed his arm. It might be a while before he fell asleep.

~~~

It was another busy night at Zentaro's. Jessalyn left the kitchen with two plates and set them in front of the customers. "Can I get you anything else?"

"No. This looks delicious," the man said.

She smiled, surveyed her tables, and froze. The creepy man from the night before sat at a table with another man—in her area.

She pasted on a smile, but inside she quaked. She approached their table, and stood where she could see both of them. She still got the shivery vibes from the first man. He had cold eyes and a colder smile. The second man's arms were crossed, and his gray gaze bounced between her and the first man as if he was gauging their reaction to each other.

"May I get either of you a drink?"

"I'll have a beer," the second said.

Creepy guy grimaced at the other man. "Your best red wine."

"Glass or the bottle?"

"Bottle."

She nodded. "I'll be right back with those."

She hurried to the bar, glad to be away from them, and put in her order. She made note of the drinks on her tablet, something she usually did while standing at the table, but had wanted to get away from the first man's leer.

At the end of the bar, Jessalyn picked up a water pitcher and strolled table to table, refilling glasses. She returned to the bar for the drinks, and served them. "Are you ready to order?" She didn't make small talk, wanting to be done with these men as soon as possible.

They placed their orders, and she hurried to the kitchen to put them in. Tammy grabbed her arms. "It's him again."

"I know. We'll have to leave the same way we did yesterday." It had been no coincidence that a car had waited outside.

"Yeah, but whose car do you think he'll disable this time?"

Theo had called his mechanic friend in the morning, and after dropping Liz at her apartment, they'd met him at her car. The spark plug wires had been pulled off. Mike had pushed them back on and the car had started right up. Jessalyn shivered every time she thought about it.

Jessalyn rubbed her forehead. "I'll text Theo."

She opened her locker, retrieved her phone, and typed. *Creepy guy is dining here again. Can you follow us home?* She shoved her phone into her purse and returned to the dining room.

Chapter 9

Theo sat on the living room couch between Bradley and Gary, watching an action movie. His phone dinged and he checked it. "What!" The creep could be the one who followed Jessa and Liz. No way would he let them go through what they had again.

Bradley paused the movie. "What's wrong?"

"That guy the girls were nervous about last night is back." He'd already told them about Jessa's car being disabled and the car chase the girls had been involved in. He stood. "I'm going over there. Either of you want to come?"

"I'm in," Gary said. "Maybe I'll recognize him."

Bradley lifted a fist. "I'll come in case you need some extra man power."

Gary raised his brows. Yeah, not the best thing to say in front of a cop. "I'll go tell Susan I'm going out. Be right back."

Gary jogged up the stairs while Theo and Bradley headed through the kitchen and got in Theo's car. He backed out of the garage, and waited for Gary. Likely, nothing would happen to Jessa while she was in the restaurant with all the customers and staff, but there was the niggling thought that the creep might follow her into the kitchen and spirit her right out the back door.

Gary hurried out and slipped into the backseat. "So, what's your plan?"

Theo closed the garage door and shrugged. "I figured we'd sit in Jessalyn's area, and order appetizers. We can keep an eye on that guy."

"If he's been arrested before, he might recognize me."

Theo tapped the steering wheel. "That might be a good thing. Maybe he'll realize he can't mess with the women at Zentaro's."

He found a spot to park and the three of them entered the restaurant.

Tammy grinned. "Mr. Argyle."

"I said you could call me Theo."

"Theo. There aren't any tables in Jessalyn's area right now. Do you want to sit somewhere else?"

He leaned on the podium. "When do you think one will vacate?"

She bit her lip. "Five minutes?"

"We'll wait." He sat on the padded bench in the waiting area, and the other men took seats on either side of him.

Gary mumbled under his breath. "I hope this doesn't turn into a situation like Susan's."

"Me, either. We were damn lucky you found her in time to do CPR and arrest her stalker." That day six months ago was etched in Theo's mind. He never again wanted to experience the fear of nearly losing a loved one to a criminal.

Two couples talked together as they exited. Theo hoped they'd been seated in Jessa's section.

Tammy peeked into the dining room then came over to Theo. "It should be a couple more minutes to clean up. It's two tables away from the scary guy." Her gaze travelled over the three of them. "Is that why you're here?"

He gave a quick nod. "We thought we'd check him out."

She glanced into the dining room, and picked up menus from behind her podium. "It's all set."

On the way to the table, Theo studied the diners. His gaze met Mansard's smirk, and he had to force himself not to freeze or go pull the man from his seat. He flipped his gaze to Tammy's back and ignored the thug—or tried to. He was sure now that Mansard still wanted Jessalyn.

At their table, Theo settled into a chair facing Mansard. "Tammy, can you have Jessalyn bring three beers?"

"Sure thing." She set the menus at each place.

Jessa came from the bar with bottles of beer and glasses, and set them down. "I'm surprised you came so early. And that you brought Bradley and Gary."

He lifted his brows, and gave her a quick side hug. "With what happened last night, I wanted backup, and I wanted a look at the guy."

"Thank you. I feel better already. Are you ordering food?" She took in the three men.

They each ordered an appetizer, and Jessa disappeared into the kitchen.

Theo leaned in. "Gary, do you know that guy with Mansard?"

"There's supposed to be a new associate from out of state. Maybe that's him." He swigged some beer from the bottle. "How do you know what Mansard looks like?"

Theo ran a hand through his hair. He'd hoped it would be weeks before having to relay anything about that evening. He explained the Friday before and paying Mitch's debt to Mansard to save Jessalyn. He left out how he told Mitch he was taking her and that Mitch's debt to him was cancelled. "So we got married in hopes it would protect her better. Looks like that might not be the case."

Bradley grinned. "Holy—"

Theo pointed at his brother. "Don't go there."

"Okay, then," Gary said. "You snatched Jessalyn right out of Mansard's jaws. I'm sure he wasn't pleased. She could have earned him much more than sixty-grand."

Any time Theo thought about what Mansard would have

done to Jessa it made him sick. Getting married wasn't enough, so he'd have to step up his protection.

"Then last night's scare. I'm sure Mansard's involved. So, what do I do?"

Gary grimaced. "You make sure she's never in a situation where she can get kidnapped, while I work with the police to take care of Mansard."

That hadn't worked out well for Autumn, even with a bodyguard. Then Susan had gone in and rescued her daughter knowing she wouldn't likely survive.

Theo ran his hand through his hair again. "That's easier said than done. I bought Jessalyn a car so she wouldn't hike to a bus stop like she threatened. Who knows what would have happened on her way there. And she was excited that she could drive herself to and from work and school without putting anyone out. She's going to be upset that I'll be following her home from work from now on."

Jessalyn approached with their dishes and passed them out. "So, are you all staying until closing?"

Theo fished his keys from his pocket and set them in front of Gary. "No. I'll stay and ride home with you. Bradley and Gary can leave after we eat."

She rested her hand on his shoulder, but it was gone before he could take hold of it. "Okay. Thanks."

After she left, Bradley leaned forward and whispered. "You haven't done the deed yet, have you?"

"You're acting immature. That doesn't rate an answer." He picked up a stuffed jalapeño from his plate and bit half of it.

Bradley chuckled. "That means you haven't. Is she sleeping on the couch in your sitting room?"

Theo ignored his stare, finished off the jalapeño and picked up another.

"Or maybe you are. No." Bradley tipped his beer glass. "She's in your bed, but you haven't touched her."

Theo shook his head. Maybe his brother should be an interrogator for the police department. He'd always been able to read him—better than their father ever could.

Gary cleared his throat. "We don't need to discuss Theo's love life or lack of." He finished a small pizza slice in four bites. "I'll check to see if we have any new information on Mansard."

"Thanks." Theo kept a covert eye on Mansard. Every time Jessa entered the room, the man tracked her. If he thought it would do any good, Theo would have gone over and punched the guy, but then Gary would have to arrest him for assault. Every so often, the man with Mansard turned enough so he was staring at Jessa. They were definitely discussing her. His chest constricted.

Before they finished their snack, Mansard had paid his bill and headed to the exit.

Gary tossed his napkin on the table. "I'll go see what car they're driving. Maybe get a plate number."

Gary waited until Mansard had pushed the door open then took off at a fast pace, following.

Bradley tapped his thumb to each of his fingers and spread his hand wide. "Five days. You've been married for five days and haven't done the deed with your wife yet." He shook his head.

"We're not talking about this." There hadn't been a time that Theo had wanted to strangle his younger brother more.

Bradley leaned forward and stage whispered. "I can tell you how to do it."

Now he imagined his fist slamming into Bradley's face.

Jessa stopped beside him. "Do what?"

Theo wrapped an arm around her waist, causing her to step closer to keep her balance. "Nothing. He thinks he's funny."

She glanced at Mansard's empty table. "Have you noticed how the atmosphere is lighter in here since that guy left? Or maybe it's just me."

Theo studied her. She did seem less tense now that Mansard was gone. "That's George Mansard."

She paled and a tremor shook her body. Her gaze flicked to Bradley and back to him. "Bradley knows about him?"

Theo stood, and wrapped his other arm around her then whispered for her ears only. "He and Gary know I paid off Mansard to prevent him from taking you, and that we married to keep it that way." But it hadn't stopped Mansard from wanting to get his paws on Jessa.

She dropped her forehead to his chest. "So they know it's fake."

He lifted her head with the side of his finger under her chin. "It's not fake. So we did it backwards. Married first then dating. I'm really attracted to you, and I don't regret this."

"Me, too." Which probably meant she was attracted to him. He hoped.

He gave her an all too short kiss. "I think you've got customers staring."

She reddened and pushed away from him. "Oh."

He smiled and sat.

Bradley tipped his glass in a salute. "It looks like you know what you're doing."

He sure hoped he did.

Gary strode back in, sat, and took a long drink from his beer bottle. "Fortunately, the other guy drove. Out of state plates. Now we know Mansard's new buddy is Omar Maestri. I'll check him out later. I took a picture of his car to show Jessalyn."

A few minutes later, Jessa came back. "You guys want another drink?"

"I'll have a Coke," Theo said. "Gary's got a picture to show you."

She scooted closer to Gary, and he showed her his phone. "Is this the car from last night?"

She shook her head. "No. That one was black."

"Thanks." Gary looked at Theo. "If any car is waiting when you two leave, go back inside and call me. I'll send a patrol car over."

"We will," Theo said.

Gary glanced at Bradley. "You ready to go?"

"Yeah." He stood. "See you two later."

Jessa stacked the dishes. "I'll be back with your drink."

Theo answered some work emails on his phone while he waited for Jessa's shift to end. After the last customer left, he sat in the waiting area in front so the dining room could be cleaned.

Before long the three women were ready to go. He stood. "Where do you two live?"

They gave their addresses.

"Okay. Tammy, you live closest, so you go first. Liz will follow you, and we'll bring up the rear. We'll wait until you're inside, then follow Liz to her place."

They couldn't do this every night. Hopefully, it would be taken care of soon. He opened the door and stood in the doorway, surveying the parking lot and street. Three cars sat at the edge of the lot, and the street was empty. Maybe Mansard expected Theo to stick around until closing and figured it was a lost cause to come back.

"Let's go, ladies."

They hurried to the cars.

Jessa held her keys up. "You want to drive?"

"You can drive. Unless you really don't want to." He wouldn't mind driving her car, but wanted, when possible, for her to have choices.

She angled for the driver's side, and he got in the passenger seat. The doors of the other women's cars closed, and both vehicles fired up. Jessa's car purred to life. At least that wouldn't be an issue tonight.

By the time they drove into the garage, it had been a long

night.

A light was on in the living room, and Gary joined them as they passed by. "No problems?"

Theo wrapped an arm around Jessa. "No one there this time. We followed the other women home to make sure."

"Good." Gary patted Theo's shoulder. "See you in the morning." He took the steps two at a time, taking a right at the landing.

Theo and Jessa took the left.

She hit the bathroom first while Theo stripped to his underwear, dropping his clothes into the hamper. He sat on the bed until Jessa came back out and took his turn in the bathroom.

Jessa was huddled under the covers when he got into bed. He pulled her into his arms without thinking. After waking with her in his arms for the past few mornings and falling asleep holding her the night before, he didn't want it any other way.

He kissed her forehead. "Goodnight, Jessa." He sure hoped he was doing this correctly. They were still a long way from a real marriage, but at least they seemed to be moving in the right direction.

She wiggled and threw her leg over his, her heat pressing against his thigh. She was too relaxed to be awake, and he was anything but relaxed. Someday soon, he hoped.

Chapter 10

Jessalyn's heart skipped a beat when Theo took his regular Friday seat in her section. With no school that day, she'd gotten up late and hadn't seen him before he left for work. Two nights in a row, she'd slept in his arms, feeling so safe that she'd relaxed quickly and nodded off. She didn't want to sleep away from him anymore.

As soon as she finished putting in her order she rushed to Theo's side.

"Hi."

He smiled. "Like old times. Almost." He tugged her closer then kissed her—too short, but sweet. "I'll give you my order in case you have to run off." He handed her the menu.

"Let me guess." She tapped her lip. "Last time, you had breaded pork cutlets, so…lasagna?"

His eyebrows went up. "I'm that predictable?"

She grinned. "Am I right?"

He grimaced. "Yes." He snatched back the menu and opened it. "But I should choose something else to be different." He pointed to an item. "Is this Steak Tagliata new?"

"It's been on the menu for about a month. I'm sure you'll like it." She hoped he didn't think she implied that he was stodgy or old by noticing his predictability.

Theo handed the menu back. "I'll take it."

She entered his order in her tablet and slipped the tablet into her pocket.

He took her hand. "Now, the big question. Will you go out with me tomorrow?"

Despite their being married already, he still seemed to want to make up for them not having dated. "I'd love to do something tomorrow. At least until I have to go to work. What did you have in mind?"

"How about a boat ride?"

"You have a friend with a boat?"

"*I* have a boat. Well, the family does. And nobody else will be at the lake house this weekend. We could put together a lunch and leave early."

"Which lake?" She shouldn't feel nervous and excited about going someplace secluded with him. They spent every night alone in his suite.

"Orchid Lake."

"Nice name. I've never heard of it."

He shrugged. "There are a lot of lakes. It's a little over an hour from here."

"Okay. It sounds fun. Sorry, but I have to make the rounds of my tables."

The evening passed quickly. Jessalyn took her dinner break with Theo, which she thoroughly enjoyed. Normally, she would sit in a corner of the kitchen, sometimes chatting with the kitchen staff or the other waitresses as they came in for their order.

Liz and Tammy decided they wanted an escort to their cars, but wanted to drive home alone. Theo agreed, with the stipulation that if someone followed them, they would drive to the police station. He also asked that they call him once they were safely inside their apartments.

The quartet left the building together, and Theo waited until Tammy and Liz left the parking lot before getting into his own car. Jessalyn felt reassured, seeing him behind her on the drive home.

This would be her seventh night sleeping at his house and it already felt like home. Theo had to be the reason because the huge house was intimidating. After she and Mitch had moved from their parents' house, it had taken months for her to consider their apartment home.

She pulled into the garage space Theo had given up for her as he took the spot at the end. They got out of their cars and went up to their room.

Jessalyn pulled out her pajamas, but he stopped her before she entered the bathroom. "I'd like you to reconsider quitting Zentaro's."

She glared at him. "I already told you I wouldn't."

He lightly held her arms. "That was before Mansard took interest in you again, and you were followed after work. The only way I know you're safe is if I escort you home every night."

"You don't have to do that."

He hugged her closer. "I'd worry from the time you left the restaurant until you got home. *If* you got home. So, if you insist on working there, I'll make sure you get here safely."

She had some guilt for his having to come out so late to protect her, but it wasn't enough to make her give up her independence. It had been his choice to involve himself in her life, and he'd have to live with the inconvenience.

He leaned back and looked her in the eye. "You could come work for AAJ. Full days on the off days from school, and a couple of hours on school days. You'll earn more than at Zentaro's and be safe."

"I can't work at your company. That's nepotism."

He grinned. "How do you think I'm CEO and Bradley is a VP? You're smart. You'll do fine as an administrative assistant."

Jessalyn backed away, put one hand on her hip and pointed at him. "You are not giving me a job." She turned her finger on herself. "I got the job at Zentaro's myself and I'm keeping it."

He sighed. "I just want to keep you safe."

Remorse set in, only for a few seconds. He spent time with her before she went into Zentaro's on the weekends and took off work to spend with her on weekdays. If she worked for him, their hours would better coordinate. But she couldn't be beholden to him for more. This was a choice she could make.

He pulled her back into his arms and kissed the side of her head. Even though she disagreed with him, he didn't get angry, but seemed resigned. He was not the controlling, wealthy man he seemed that first day.

"I'll think about it," she said.

~~~

Saturday dawned sunny and warm. Theo didn't have his morning swim since he figured he'd jump in the lake. Although he untangled himself from Jessa, he stayed in bed, waiting for her to wake up. He hadn't been happy with how they'd ended their night and took hope from her cuddling him in her sleep that she wasn't still mad at him.

They'd been married a week and had yet to consummate it. They had grown comfortable with each other, so it didn't bother him too much.

Jessa's eyes fluttered and she stretched. She froze when her gaze landed on him. "Morning."

He took her hand. "Good morning. Can you forgive me for being overly protective?"

She glanced at his bare chest, then her gaze veered to their joined hands. "I'm not surprised since that's how we started."

"Jessa, I care about your safety." He planted his hand in the middle of her back and pulled her close. "I care about you more now than I did a week ago." Much more.

She tipped her head back and stared into his eyes. A myriad of emotions flitted across her face. "You care about me?"

"Of course, I care about you. Do you think I'd marry any

woman who needed protection? It's you."

"You don't regret getting married?"

He'd tried to tell her with his actions that she was important to him, not wanting to scare her by saying anything. "No. Never." He bracketed her head between his hands and stared intently into her eyes. "This marriage started as a way for me to protect you, but it's more than that to me." He kissed her forehead, wishing he could kiss her lips, but now wasn't the time.

She sighed, her body relaxing.

He nuzzled her neck. "You ready to get up so we can start our ocean voyage?"

She laughed. "I thought you said this boat was at a lake house."

"I did, but it's a big lake." He scooted away from her before he did something she wasn't ready for. He felt her watching him as he headed to the bathroom, liking that she did it.

~~~

Jessalyn walked beside Theo. He held her hand and carried a cooler in the other. She liked how he seemed to unconsciously touch her, even when nobody was around. There was an unmistakable attraction between them. She wished they'd had a few pre-marriage dates, getting to know each other with no pressure and no expectations. She believed Theo when he said he cared for her, but didn't know if he was trying to force himself to fall for her to make the best of the situation he'd gotten himself into, or if he really was. His saying he wouldn't have married someone else to offer protection had to mean he had strong feelings.

She glanced over her shoulder at the lake house. It had huge windows on this side, all the better to see the view. The vacation house was bigger than the house her parents had owned.

She stumbled, and Theo caught her around the waist.

He chuckled. "You know, it's easier to walk if you're watching where you're going."

She giggled. "But your house is beautiful."

"I'll show it to you after the boat ride."

"Okay." She regarded the dock they approached, and the— "Wow. I expected a speed boat, not a cabin cruiser."

"This is a speed boat, but it sleeps six, too."

"Do you sleep on it?"

"I haven't in years. When I was growing up, we had one similar to this and a few times my parents trailered the boat to other lakes for vacations."

"That sounds fun."

"Looking back on it, it was. At the time, I wanted to go back home and play video games with my friends and spend time with them." He squeezed her hand. "If we hadn't gone, I would have missed out on a lot of time with my mom."

Jessalyn dragged him to a stop, and wrapped her arms around his waist, dropping her head to his chest. "It's hard losing your mom when you still need her."

The cooler hit the ground and he pulled her into a tighter hug. It was a sad thing to have in common. "At least I still had my dad. He tried hard to make up for our loss. I'm sorry you didn't have that."

She rubbed her cheek on his shirt. "We were so busy making sure we did well in school and hiding the fact we had no parents, that it wasn't until late in the evenings that I felt the loss." She held him for a moment longer then pushed away. "You promised me a boat ride."

They resumed walking, and when they stepped onto the dock, their footfalls echoed across the water. Theo expertly jumped onto the boat then helped her aboard.

She followed him inside. "What a cute little kitchen."

He stored the cooler under the table. "It's called a galley."

He patted a door. "And this is the head, meaning bathroom to landlubbers." He pointed to the end. "And that's sleeping quarters. Maybe next time we'll use it."

She raised her eyebrows. "You want to spend the night here?"

He grinned. "I wasn't thinking about sleeping."

"Oh." Her cheeks heated, and she looked down, hoping he didn't notice. Each time they kissed, the closer she was to telling him yes to having sex. But she wasn't ready for it yet.

He strode to the steps. "Let's go topside."

Jessalyn stepped onto the deck.

Theo patted a chair. "Have a seat while I cast off."

She would have asked if she could help, but he was already striding off.

A few minutes later, he sat at the wheel, and the boat roared to life. He grinned as he moved a lever and they glided away from the dock.

The only boat with a motor Jessalyn had been on before was one where her brother had sat at the back and steered by turning the motor. Mitch had borrowed it from a friend, and they'd cruised for a couple of hours around a small lake with a tiny island near the middle.

Theo yanked his shirt off and tossed it down the stairs. She'd come prepared, so did the same, revealing her bikini top.

He scrutinized her, his gaze traveling up and down her body. Her breath caught in her throat. She didn't know how he could have such an effect on her. And that sexy grin gave her tingles between her legs. Hopefully, he thought her blush was from the sun.

She leaned back in her seat and took in the sights. Houses were in clusters with long expanses of forest between. Most houses had docks and beaches. A breeze carried the scent of pine. "How long have you been here?"

"We've been on the lake for thirty years."

She laughed. "You're not thirty."

"My dad bought the house before I was born. But we've only been in this house for about six months."

She narrowed her eyes. "How come you moved from the first house?"

He stared for so long, she didn't think he'd answer. "You don't know?"

So much for an answer. "I guess not."

"Do you remember that serial killer case last year?"

Her heart pounded at his bringing it up. "Yes. It was horrible. All those women." She'd felt relieved and guilty for not being a target since her hair wasn't red.

His hands tightened on the steering wheel. "The killer was married to Susan. He committed the…crimes in our old lake house."

"Oh, my God." Jessalyn covered her mouth with her hand. That was why Susan looked vaguely familiar. She must have been in the news. The thought that she'd been unknowingly married to a killer brought tears to her eyes. "That must have been tough for your whole family."

Jessalyn left her seat and stood next to him. He wrapped an arm around her waist, and she gave him a hug.

Theo kissed her collarbone. "We got through it together."

Like she and Mitch had gotten through the deaths of their parents and living on their own as teens together. Until he sold her to protect himself. Theo had saved her life from someone she'd always trusted. She hugged him again and kissed his cheek.

He raised an eyebrow, but she shook her head then stared through the windshield.

Theo eased the speed down. "I thought you might like to try tubing."

"Floating down a river on an inner tube?"

He smiled. "That's one way to do it. But we tie a tube to the back of the boat and tow it."

"Is that safe?"

"Autumn loves it, and Susan wouldn't let her do something dangerous."

"Okay. I'll give it a try."

Theo shut off the engine and went to the back of the boat. He extracted a folded up vinyl from under a bench seat, then inflated the tube and attached a rope to it. The tube had two large handles on top and a solid piece of vinyl filling the center hole. He tossed it into the water then tied the other end of the rope to the back of the boat.

He straightened up. "There you go. You can kneel in it and hold the handles. I'll go slow at first until you get used to it."

He pulled a life jacket from the compartment. "And you should wear this."

Jessalyn took off her shorts and glanced at Theo when he made a strangled sound.

He stared at her bikini bottoms, then up at her face. "You are so beautiful."

Her heart fluttered at the adoration on his face. "So are you." She dropped her gaze to the deck as she slipped on the jacket. She couldn't believe she'd said that, but he was. She'd thought it the first time she'd seen him.

Theo buckled and adjusted the strap for her, then helped her onto the tube, and positioned her hands over the grips. He gave her a quick kiss, then propelled the tube away from the boat. She kind of wished he'd haul her back in and give her another kiss.

He stood with his hands on his hips as she drifted farther away. "You ready?"

She bit her lip. "I think so."

He scrambled onto the deck and started the engine. After a glance back, the motor got louder and the boat moved. The rope slowly uncurled until it was taut, and she started to glide forward.

So far, it was okay. She was in the wake of the boat with no waves. Theo kept checking on her and increasing speed. He took a slow turn and the tube bounced over the wake. She held on tighter as water splashed in her face. She couldn't let go to wipe her eyes, so she blinked a few times. She passed over the wake again and was in the smooth water behind the boat. Theo turned the other way and she flew over the wake again. More water covered her face. Jessalyn could see how Autumn would have fun with this, especially if the boat went faster, but she wasn't a fan. Once she was in the calm behind the boat again, she released the handles and slid into the cool water.

The life jacket kept her high in the waves with hardly any paddling. The boat motor slowed to an idle, and Theo spun the boat around and stopped alongside her. "Hey, what happened?"

"I decided I didn't really like it, so I let go." She hoped he didn't think she was a spoilsport for not liking something he planned for her.

He put a ladder over the side, and she climbed halfway up before he lifted her the rest of the way and set her in front of him. "That's all right. Susan doesn't really like it either, but she'll go sometimes when Autumn asks her to double with her."

He took the life jacket off her and tossed it aside. He drew her into his arms and kissed her. His warm body against her cold one, and sunshine on her back, heated her in seconds. His lips nibbled to her jaw and down her neck, sending delicious shivers through her. His hand slipped down her back and over her butt, pulling her closer, showing her how much he wanted her. Being in his arms like this had her forgetting everything, and made her want more.

Theo showed his caring concern in everything he did. Her body called out for his touch everywhere. If he suggested they go to the sleeping quarters, she'd gladly follow.

"Whoot! Whoot! Whoot!" A group of teen boys' voices

broke through her lusty thoughts.

She opened her eyes. A small speedboat passed with several boys in it, two with double thumbs in the air.

Her face heated, and she wondered how far down her body the red went.

Theo chuckled. "Let's eat lunch."

"Umm. Sure." There was something else she'd been more hungry for, but the moment had been lost.

He pointed to the cushions in back. "Why don't you sit, and I'll get the food."

He returned with the cooler. "I have to haul the tube in." He kissed her forehead and smiled. "You made me forget."

It pleased her that she affected him, too. She unloaded the sandwiches, potato salad, and drinks while Theo coiled up the rope and set the tube on the deck.

After they ate lunch, Theo picked her up and jumped into the lake. She screamed until her head went under. At least she'd closed her mouth in time. She came up and wiped her eyes. He tread water next to her and grinned.

It was more of a shock because she'd been unprepared. "Why did you do that?"

He swam a circle around her, but she spun to face him, worried he'd duck her under.

"I wanted to swim."

She could say something about him not giving her a choice about swimming, but he was in too good of a mood to spoil it. She started swimming toward shore, not sure which way the house was. It didn't matter anyway since she'd never reach the beach.

Theo glided in beside her, matching her strokes.

She glanced at him. "You can go at your own pace. I don't mind swimming alone."

"I'm not leaving your side. I'll get in some faster laps after you're back on the boat."

Every thought he had seemed to be about keeping her safe. She fell a little more for him.

Her arms started to tire, so she flipped under and headed back toward the boat. Theo could probably swim ten times farther than her. He'd be a good man to have nearby if she was on a sinking ship. He was a good man to have near her all the time. Despite their rocky start, she was glad they were together.

A short distance from the boat, Theo dragged her into his arms. He kicked his legs to keep them afloat. If she kicked, too, their legs would probably tangle and they'd sink.

"I enjoy spending time with you." He kissed her cheek. "My weekends were often boring before you." His lips touched her other cheek. "And in the water, no one lets me get near enough to do…this." He pushed her under and swam away.

She came up sputtering. He was ten feet away and laughing at her.

"You…you're stealthy." She swam toward him, expecting him to swim away, but he stayed where he was. She put her hands on his shoulders, using them to lift herself up, and pushing him under. She had no doubt that he could kick hard enough to keep his head above water. She moved away, but he caught her foot while still submerged.

She screamed and kicked free, then swam as fast as she could with her remaining strength.

He burst from the water and began to pursue her. She laughed, reaching out to the ladder. He snagged her foot again and dragged her back to him. She flipped over to better see him. The corners of his mouth tipped up into not quite a smile. He slid his hands to her knee and pulled her closer. Then she was plastered to his chest, his lips on hers. She wrapped her arms around the back of his neck and kissed him. She touched her tongue to his lips and he groaned, taking her in.

Her legs had wrapped around his waist without her noticing until he pulled her hips tighter against him. The movement of his legs to keep their heads above water brushed him against her.

She moaned and he thrust his hips. They sank below the surface, separated, and came up sputtering.

Theo laughed. "You know it's your fault we sank. You made me forget everything but touching you."

Jessalyn climbed onto the bottom rung of the ladder. "My fault? You're the champion swimmer. You should be able to swim through anything." She giggled at his narrowed eyes.

He came closer and she was prepared to scramble aboard. He lifted his hands in the air. "I'm not going to pull you in." He reversed direction, floating on his back away from her.

She kept a wary eye on him as he flipped to his front and struck out in the direction they'd gone before at a much faster clip. She eased into the water again and floated around. She should have told him that her weekends were more enjoyable with him, too.

Once her fingers started to wrinkle, she climbed out of the water and lay on the back bench seat, propped up enough to watch Theo returning to the boat. His still powerful strokes brought him back at an amazing speed. Didn't the man ever tire?

Theo grabbed the ladder, then the top of the boat and swung his legs around, landing on the deck, all in one long, smooth move. He whipped his head in her direction, sending water drops over her sun-heated skin.

"Theo!"

He knelt down and kissed her, stopping all too soon. "Let's head back to the dock."

Jessalyn stayed on the back seat, worshipping the sun, while Theo started the motor, and put on some speed. He kept looking back at her.

Once Theo had tied the boat up and closed it up, he showed her the house. They'd have to stay over sometime. It was hard to imagine having enough money to own a huge vacation house that was only used on some weekends. Of course, Theo's house was four times the size. She was so outclassed, and she didn't know why Theo was even interested in her.

Chapter 11

It was always nice talking to Theo between serving customers. It was totally different from before when he was only a customer—a really sexy customer. At the end of the night she met him and the other women at the front door so they could leave together.

Theo stepped out first, and a black car waited in the street, the same as a couple nights before. He hauled them all back inside and called the police. They watched through the windows as five minutes later, a police cruiser stopped behind the car. The tires squealed in protest as the mysterious driver raced away with the police car in pursuit.

Once the road was clear, they hurried to their cars. Instead of giving her a kiss and reassuring her before getting in their cars, like she expected, Theo's eyes glared with anger, directed at her as much as the bad guy. She was nervous driving home, but not from the black car. That guy was too busy to harass her. Theo was the one who worried her at the moment.

Jessalyn drove into her garage bay, pushed the garage door button, and got out of her car. Theo slammed his car door. She hurried inside and up to their suite. She spun around, not knowing what to expect. He'd argued with worry before, but this was well beyond that. She didn't think he'd become violent, but he hadn't been like this before.

He stalked into the room, his expression stormy and voice

raised. "We can't keep doing this."

He couldn't mean them being married. The thought of them separating squeezed her heart so hard she couldn't catch her breath. "Doing what?"

Theo pointed to the front of the house and took her arm. "Coming out of your work with a car waiting for you." His voiced shook. "I married you to keep you safe. I can't do that if you insist on putting yourself in dangerous situations. You've got to quit."

"It scares me when I see that car, but we're taking precautions." She yanked her arm away from him and stalked to the bathroom, slamming the door behind her. She leaned on the counter, willing away her shaking and slowing her breathing.

Arguments with Mitch always had good reasons warranting her anger, but what Theo said made sense. It was a risk leaving work at night with that Mansard guy around, but if she quit and this situation resolved quickly, she would have quit for nothing. She'd have to search for another job, and it might not fit her schedule as well—except Theo had offered her employment with hours that would work for her. She hated taking a job because of who she was and not for what she could do. Her new coworkers might resent her for being handed a job.

Her friends. She bowed her head. They would never have been put at risk except for Mansard's interest in her. If she no longer worked at Zentaro's, they might be off his radar again.

She stood and leaned against the wall with her hands on her head. Theo seemed to want to make this marriage work. For her friends, she'd give him this, and let him enjoy being her protector.

After she got ready for bed, she stepped into the bedroom. Theo spun around. He must have been pacing, running his hands through his hair, sending it in all directions. She itched to smooth it out for him.

"I'm sorry," they said together. It was as if they'd choreographed their first words.

He strode to her, inches between them, but didn't touch her. "I was overbearing. I should have handled that differently."

She took his hand, and his shoulders relaxed. "I could only see how you were trying to control me. But you've only done it when my safety is a concern. Otherwise, you've been really sweet."

He touched the side of her neck and brushed his thumb across her cheek. "I don't want to control you, but seeing the way Mansard looks at you scares me. What if I'm not there to stop him?" He tipped his forehead to hers and closed his eyes. "I don't even want to think about what he'd do if he takes you." He let out a ragged breath.

"He scared me before I knew who he was. Can we sit down? I want to explain something."

He stepped back, her hand still in his, leading her to the sitting room.

She tugged. "No. In the bed." She'd never told anybody about what happened, mostly because it might have ruined her life. Being held close would make it easier. She hoped.

His eyebrows popped up. "What exactly do you want me to do?"

She bit her lip and stared at their hands. "Hold me while we talk. You can be dressed how you normally are for bed." She wanted that extra warmth to help her through it. She slipped her hand out of his and dove under the covers, then leaned her back against the headboard.

He kept his gaze locked on her as he jerked his shirt over his head and dropped it on the floor. He paused with his hand on his belt buckle.

She'd never watched him undress before. He'd done it while she was in the bathroom, and when she exited, she kept her focus on the bed. She realized she was staring at that hand, and her gaze flew to his face. He had a half-smile.

The buckle clinked when he unlatched it. The button on

his jeans popped open, and he lowered his zipper as if he had all night to undress. She'd never been to a strip club. Professional stripping probably involved a lot of provocative gyrations, but what Theo was doing to her body couldn't have been any different than the response a stripper expected.

Her temperature must have spiked. She'd love to throw back the covers to cool off, but that would tell him how much he affected her. Of course, her fast breathing would give it away. At least he couldn't tell how much her lower anatomy wanted him to touch it.

His pants slid down his legs and he stepped out of them. Unfortunately, she could tell how much *his* lower anatomy wanted her. That wasn't what this should have been about right now. Try as she might, her body wasn't listening to her, but was responding to his desire.

He slipped into the bed. "You better start talking, or I won't be able to keep my promise."

She tipped her head. "Promise?"

He kissed her forehead. "Not to make love to you until you say so."

She stared at her clasped hands, and Theo covered them with one of his, giving a little squeeze. For a moment, she wanted to give in, but she needed to talk to him first. "After our parents died, Mitch and I were going to be carted off to social services because our aunt didn't want us."

"How old was Mitch?"

"Seventeen." She balled her hand into a fist. Theo uncurled her fingers, flattening her hand over his heart with his hand covering hers.

She blew out a long breath. "He said if we weren't assigned to the same foster family, he'd run away. Anyway, he convinced our aunt to sign the papers to say we were living with her, but we weren't going to. He had to give her a third of the proceeds from the house when it sold, but we got all the insurance money."

Theo's hand tightened on hers. "Greedy, heartless woman."

"Yeah. We got forty thousand in insurance, and after splitting the house money, we got another fifty thousand. Mitch graduated before the house sale closed, and we moved to an apartment. We couldn't tell our friends we were living on our own, or the wrong people might have found out and separated us. By the time Mitch graduated college, the money had run out. I had after school jobs from the time I was sixteen."

"Didn't Mitch work?"

"Yes. What I'm getting to is that we discussed every decision. Where we moved, what we bought, our jobs. I'm used to being part of the decision-making."

"You weren't part of the decision-making when he tried to trade you to Mansard."

The anger toward her brother made her boil. Mitch had been her protector, but that all changed when he tried to sell her. She would have been in the arms of dozens of men over the last two weeks instead of being with a man who cared for her. She shivered, and Theo held her closer then tucked the blanket under her chin.

"Let me start again," he said. "I'd like you to consider working fewer nights. That reduces your risk with Mansard and lets us spend more time together. Living here, you don't have to pay for rent or food, so you can keep your whole paycheck. You'll still end up with more money for yourself."

This wasn't really about the money anymore, but she liked how Theo framed his argument to include one of her previous concerns. "Okay." She lifted her head to watch him. "I'll quit Zentaro's and come work for your company." She still hated the nepotism but knew she could do the job.

She'd never seen him with such a big smile.

He kissed her forehead. "Thank you. It means a lot to me that you're doing this for both of us."

She liked the way he said that. It was for both of them and not just her. "Yes. My boss may have to hire someone, so it might not happen right away."

"We'll deal with it." He framed her face between his hands and kissed her.

She turned toward him and wrapped her arms around his neck. She didn't want to talk anymore. "I want you to make love to me." She couldn't believe she'd actually said it.

He pulled her into a tight hug. "Are you sure?"

"I'm sure." She wouldn't tell him how nervous she was.

He gave her a scorching kiss, then stripped off her tank top. He slid her down so they were lying on the bed. His kisses grew hotter when one hand caressed her breast. Falling asleep in Theo's arms had made her crave his touch.

She ran her hand down his chest and he groaned as she passed over his nipple. She liked the way the sound vibrated through his chest, so she rubbed it again.

Her pajama shorts disappeared as if by magic, and Theo's fingers explored between her legs. She didn't know the pleasure could build to an intense level so fast. Heat filled her body, and she couldn't catch her breath. An orgasm took her by surprise, and she dug her nails into his ribs, screaming into his mouth.

Before Jessalyn's breathing returned to normal, Theo had shucked his boxer-briefs and retrieved a condom from the bedside table. He rolled it on and positioned himself over her.

He gave her quick little kisses that weren't nearly satisfying enough. He was poised at her entrance. "You ready for more?"

It melted her heart that he gave her a chance to change her mind. If her vagina could speak, it would be yelling, *Come in already*. She grabbed his butt. "Yes."

He probed and slid in an inch. She strained to drag him closer, but he resisted, going at his own pace, and she didn't have a choice. The one time that she didn't care. She wrapped her legs around him and ran her hands up his back. His drugging kisses divided her attention until he was fully seated. She

101

threw back her head and gasped.

Theo kissed her neck. "You okay?"

"Don't stop!"

He chuckled and pulled back, then plunged in again. She caught the rhythm and met him with each thrust. Her fantasies of sex with Theo paled in comparison to how amazing it was for real. She spiraled higher and higher—more than the first time. Her breathing couldn't keep up, but breathing wasn't important at the moment. Then her whole body exploded into a million sizzling fragments. She screamed, but he caught it with a kiss.

Theo stiffened and groaned into the pillow. He held her tighter for a few moments longer then rolled beside her. "Be right back." He got up and returned seconds later, tucking her next to him.

Skin-to-skin with Theo without sex was nearly as good as with.

He nuzzled her neck. "That was make-up sex."

She wiggled her hips. "Does that mean it won't usually be that good?"

"Mmm. No doubt, it'll get better. We'll learn what the other likes."

She flushed at the thought that anything could top what they'd just done.

He kissed her cheek, as if he couldn't get enough of her. "Now let's get to sleep. We've got a big day tomorrow."

Theo turned the bedside light off. A few moments later, he groaned. "I'll never get to sleep like this." Her thigh was over his stomach, her heat against his hip. He flipped her around, spooning her, then dropped his arm over her waist.

He thought that was better? How was she supposed to sleep with his half hard nakedness pressed against her butt? She drifted off with the thought that she was exactly where she should be.

Chapter 12

Theo leaned back in his chair, elbows on the armrest, fingertips steepled. Sunlight streamed in the large windows of his fifth floor office. He'd had two glorious weeks with Jessa since they'd first made love. Although he'd cared for her, his feelings had grown into love as they got physically closer. He hoped she felt the same.

Their second time on the boat, he'd coaxed her into the cabin where they'd made love. Once they docked, she'd eagerly followed him to his room at the lake house. Their honeymoon activities might have been delayed, but they were making up for lost time.

He hadn't known what to expect when he rushed into marriage, but the contentment and happiness he now experienced took him by surprise. He picked up the five-by-seven picture on his desk, one of the wedding pictures Alex had forwarded to him. He and Jessa had been repeating the final wedding vows, and if he didn't know better, he would have guessed they were in love. Her soft expression and his—he'd been half in love with her that day.

His desk phone buzzed, and his admin's voice on the speaker broke the silence. "Your two o'clock is here. Mitch Waters."

"Thanks, Elise. Send him in."

He hadn't been sure if Mitch would show for the appointment since Theo hadn't given the man a reason for the meeting.

Mitch sauntered in and sat in the chair across from Theo. "What's this about?"

Theo scooted forward "I thought I'd—"

Mitch jumped up and pointed to Theo's hand. "You're married? You were already married when you bought my sister?"

Theo growled. "You were selling her to a pimp, and it matters that I'm married?"

Mitch ran a hand over his face. "I…" His gaze fell to his feet before meeting Theo's stare. "I screwed up so much, but I do care what happens to her."

Theo grinned. "Then you should be happy to know that I married Jessalyn."

Mitch dropped into the chair. "No kidding?"

"Same day you left her with me." He turned around the picture he'd been staring at and wondered if Mitch saw the same thing Theo had. He set the frame down and leaned forward. "That doesn't mean what you did was right. If I'd come in five minutes later, she'd be God knows where, being sexually abused."

Mitch paled.

Whenever Theo thought about how close Jessa had come to having her life destroyed, his whole body knotted up. He rolled his shoulders and shoved the disturbing thoughts away. "That's not why I asked you here."

Mitch gripped the arms of his chair. "Okay. Why?"

"Someday Jessa's—"

"Jessa?"

Theo shrugged. "My nickname for her. Anyway, someday Jessa's going to forgive you, and I'd like you to be more established by then." And the success would ensure Mitch would never have a reason to use Jessalyn as payment again—but he wouldn't mention that.

He leaned forward, his eyes wide. "You think she'll forgive

me?"

"She told me how you took care of her after your parents died. I think, eventually, that will overcome her anger over this incident."

Mitch sighed. "I sure hope so."

"I'd like to offer you some assistance." Mitch's exuberance and beginning plans for his renewable energy device had convinced Theo to invest in the project. If he'd kept in touch with Mitch and offered business advice, Mitch might not have needed to go to Mansard, exposing Jessalyn to the loan shark.

Mitch's brows rose. "More than paying my debt and forgiving what I owe you?"

"Like I said, it's for Jessa. What I propose is providing an agent to represent you and your prototype to manufacturers. I don't build entire systems, just the electronics, so I can't manufacture it for you." If a satisfactory agreement was brokered, Mitch wouldn't get into trouble that would affect Jessa again.

"But I want to do this myself." The man's single-mindedness could mean a well funded company, might bring a similar product to market well before Mitch's.

"You don't have the experience or the money to manufacture this yourself."

"I built a prototype. It took time and money to get it right. I don't want to turn it over to someone else."

Theo understood the possessiveness. This was Mitch's idea. As far as he knew, no one else had come up with this yet.

"All the better. Having a working prototype gives you more leverage. An agent will approach renewable energy manufacturers, present your device, and get a good deal for you. Probably some kind of profit sharing. If you tried it on your own, they'd want to buy it outright, and you'd be out of the picture."

Mitch gripped the chair arms. "Yeah, but once they see it, they can design their own."

"Don't you have a patent on it?"

Mitch grimaced. "I applied for one. It's pending."

"Good. Any manufacturer would be crazy to start from scratch if they could get you and your design for a good deal immediately. It would be years down the road before they had a working model with their own design. With you, they'd be making money within a few months."

Mitch crossed his arms and lifted his chin. "I won't sell if I don't like the deal they wanted to make."

"Of course not."

Mitch squinted, likely ticking off his options. "I don't know how to find that kind of agent."

"I have one in mind. I can set up an appointment for you, if you'd like."

"I'll talk to him, but if I don't like what I hear, I'm out of there."

"That's all I ask." Theo stood and held his hand out. "You won't regret it."

Mitch sprung to his feet and shook Theo's hand. "I don't know why you're trying to help me."

"We're family now." Theo wanted his wife to be happy and that included helping her reestablish a relationship with her brother. He picked up a business card from his desk and held it out to Mitch. "You've got an appointment Tuesday at three o'clock. Here's the info."

Mitch took the card and glanced at it. "Katherine Hanley? A woman?"

"You don't think a woman can do the job?"

Mitch scratched his head. "Um. Sure."

Theo grinned. "She's one of the best. You'll see."

"All right." He flicked the card. "I'll give it a shot. Thanks, man."

After Mitch left, Theo sat and leaned back, lacing his hands behind his head. His life was headed toward perfect.

In less than three hours, he'd be taking Jessa to Zentaro's

for dinner instead of having her serve him.

He snatched up his phone and sent her a text. *I can hardly wait to have dinner with you tonight.*

A few minutes later, he got her response. *Me either, but you're distracting me from work. I hear my boss's boss is a tyrant.*

He chuckled. *He'd probably order you to his office and kiss you senseless, then send you back to work unsatisfied.*

She sent him a kiss-face emoticon.

~~~

Jessalyn pulled into the student parking lot at the college. She'd been driving herself for almost a month and still couldn't believe she owned a Mustang. It wasn't much like her father's, but she still felt closer to him when she drove it. Theo had been so right when he thought she'd like the stick shift.

She climbed out, shoved her purse into her backpack and slung it over her shoulder.

A guy got out of a beat up black sports car beside her. "Sweet ride."

She grinned. "Thanks."

He glanced back at his car. "I wish I had rich parents."

She lifted her left hand and wiggled the fingers. "A gift from my husband." She hoped that didn't make it sound like she married him for his money. What a joke that was when she'd had little choice.

He fell in beside her as they walked toward the buildings. "You married an old dude?"

She laughed. "He's not thirty yet." That made her realize she didn't know when Theo's birthday was. She'd have to ask Susan.

They split paths when she veered off to go to the nursing building. He waved. "See you around."

"Sure." After a few steps, a strange prickle irritated her neck. It felt like someone was watching her. She glanced toward the guy she'd walked with, but he was taking determined strides away from her. She quickened her pace and rubbed her neck.

Once she reached the building her class was in, she sat on a step and retied her shoe. She gave a surreptitious glance around, but didn't see anyone staring at her. Students were heading to class like normal. She could still feel it. Maybe she was being paranoid—seeing Mansard and the black car too many times. No one could kidnap her from the campus with so many people around.

Her three classes passed quickly with a short break for lunch. She left the last class with Sally by her side. The pretty, green eyed blonde always rushed around as if she was late for something. Before Jessalyn had her car, they'd had to hurry out to catch the bus after their last class. Otherwise there was a twenty minute wait for the following one.

"I really appreciate you dropping me off, Jessalyn."

Jessalyn laughed. "You've said that every single day since I got my car. You're two blocks out of the way. It's no big deal." They walked in silence for a few minutes, and that prickly feeling at the back of her neck bothered her again. "Does it feel like someone's watching us?"

Sally narrowed her eyes. "I hadn't noticed." She slowed a bit. "I don't know." She looked over one shoulder then stopped and turned around. "I don't see anyone staring at us."

Jessalyn stopped and studied their surroundings. "I felt it earlier and didn't see anyone." She hadn't told Sally about the guy who tried to buy her, or that he'd been staring at her in the restaurant.

Most people strode with purpose. The one coming toward the parking lot was a guy she'd seen nearly every day she'd parked here, and he had a backpack like a student. He strode past them and kept going. A man, older than the traditional student, sat on a bench talking on a phone. He was probably in his late thirties. It would be easy enough for him to watch her.

Another man sat with his back against a tree, staring at his phone. She hadn't noticed him when they passed. Another guy looked all around. It could have been him, trying to act like he hadn't been watching. Then a girl came up, kissed him, and they walked away with their arms around each other's waists.

"What do you think?" Jessalyn asked.

"Nothing really. Maybe you imagined it."

"Yeah, maybe." Jessalyn dragged in a breath. Probably nobody was watching. At least, not with sinister intent. Jessalyn beeped the locks as they approached the car, and she got in a second after Sally did. After this, she'd pay more attention to who was around her.

All this worry because her brother had selfishly tried to use her to pay off his loan. She wanted a normal, non-scary life again, but with Theo—the wonderful part of her new life.

~~~

The following week, Jessalyn arrived at school and headed for her class. That prickly sensation sent a warning through her body. She checked her surroundings as well as she could without making it obvious. Everybody seemed to be going somewhere and not paying attention to her.

Beside the door to the building, she leaned her back to the wall and pulled out her phone, pretending to send a text. She kept her head down and searched. There. The older man she'd seen last time sat on the same bench, reading a book. She took a picture of him. He glanced up, catching her eye. Even from this far away, a wave of revulsion passed through her. He had to be the one, but was he associated with George Mansard? She could be over-sensitive.

A group of students approached, and she entered the building with them, finally feeling safe.

The rest of her day was normal. Even when she had to leave the nursing building for her second class, she didn't sense anyone watching.

As she was leaving the last class with Sally, Professor Donovan cleared his throat. "Jessalyn and Sally, could I talk with you for a minute?"

The women looked at each other and shrugged. Jessalyn didn't have any outstanding problems with the class and was pretty sure Sally didn't.

"Sure, Professor." Jessalyn stopped in front of him with Sally at her side.

The professor sat on the edge of his desk. "I've been asked to find some students willing to talk to a group of philanthropists for a new scholarship program for nursing students. You two were on the list of students who weren't carrying a full load, and I'm guessing that was for financial reasons."

Jessalyn wished she'd had something like that when she started nursing school. She'd be done by now if she had. They hadn't discussed it, but she knew Theo would insist on paying for her remaining schooling. She wasn't a student in need any longer, but maybe she could help some others. "Who would we have to talk to, and what would we tell them?"

"Some are regular contributors and some are new. Just tell them your experiences with financial hardship. How it's delayed you finishing school. Let them see how smart you girls are. Generally convince them how good it would be for the community to produce nurses sooner."

Jessalyn glanced at Sally. "I guess I could do that."

"Me, too." Sally nodded.

Professor Donovan grinned. "Great." He held out two invitations. "All the information is on there."

Jessalyn studied the card. "What's this address?" It wasn't a hotel or regular venue.

"That's one of the dean's houses." He stood. "Oh. This is formal, so dress your best."

"Okay," Jessalyn said. "We'll try to get these people to donate lots of money."

They exited the building, and she inspected her invitation. It was for next week on Friday. She'd have to leave the office early.

Sally sighed. "I don't have anything to wear to this. The only thing formal I have is my prom dress, and it belongs on a teenager."

"I don't even have that." Jessalyn grinned. "But I have a credit card I haven't touched yet. I'm sure Theo wouldn't mind if we use it for a good cause."

Sally stopped her. "You want to buy me a dress? I can't accept that. I'm sure I can find something nice at a resale shop."

Not long ago, she'd have been thinking the same thing. "You'll have a better dress selection at a store. You're more likely to get a dress that looks good on you and will dazzle them at this party thing. We can wow them with our confidence and how smart we are. We try to influence these philanthropists to donate tons of money for scholarships. It's like Theo is making a donation, too. Come to think of it…maybe he's already been invited." She closed her eyes for a second. "I would love to see him in a tux."

Sally laughed. "Come on, starry-eyed girl. Let's get out of here."

It wasn't until they were driving away that Jessalyn realized she hadn't noticed being stared at. Maybe she'd been too distracted by the invitation. Hopefully, that guy had been waiting for someone other than her and was gone.

Chapter 13

Jessalyn leaned over the bathroom counter and added a bit more mascara. She blinked then opened her eyes wide. Perfect. She shook her head and the curls she'd put into her blonde hair settled around her face.

She took her jade dress off the hanger and stepped into it, slithering it up her legs and hips. She slipped her arms into the short sleeves and zipped the back which finished just above her bra. The front showed a bit of cleavage. She'd brought the shoes in with her so Theo would get the full affect.

They'd had so much fun trying on dresses. Susan had taken her and Sally to the best shops and kept reminding them not to check the price tags since Theo was paying. She'd even covered half the screen when Jessalyn signed the receipt. Jessalyn hadn't found out until after getting home that her dress had cost eight-hundred dollars. It was worth more than her entire wardrobe.

She opened the door, and Theo glanced up from his phone. His eyes widened and chest expanded. "You're gorgeous." He stood and wrapped his arms around her waist. "If you weren't so set on going to this fundraiser, I'd strip off your dress and make love to you." He kissed her neck and nibbled his way to her ear. "It's going to be hard to wait until you're home again."

She shivered. Thinking about Theo all evening might make it hard to convince rich people to open their wallets. "I've got to go."

"Wait. Remember to stay aware, and if it looks like some-one's following you, go to the police station."

"I will." It had become habit to keep an eye out. She grabbed her phone from the dresser, set it for vibrate, and slipped it into a small pocket in her dress, probably intended for a lipstick or ID. She picked up the small clutch she'd bought with the dress.

Jessalyn pursed her lips and touched her fingers to them then his. "I'd kiss you except it would mess up my lipstick."

He growled and kissed her neck again. "You'll have to make up for it later."

Warmth spread through her, making her almost wish she could stay home. At the bedroom door, she remembered the invitation and ran back to the dresser for it. She hurried to the stairs, then slowed. Otherwise, she'd probably break her neck in her heels.

Bradley leaned against the kitchen counter, arms crossed, as a bag of popcorn popped in the microwave. "Don't you look beautiful? Go collect those millions."

Jessalyn gave a nervous laugh. "I'll try." In the garage, she hit her garage door button and got into her car. She drove to Sally's apartment and parked on the street in front of the four-family home. Sally lived with her mother in the upper right unit. Jessalyn got out and rounded the front of her car. A curtain moved in one of the upper windows and Sally's mother waved. Jessalyn leaned against the hood to wait for her friend.

Within a minute, Sally came out the front door in her beau-tiful royal blue gown. The women hugged, and Jessalyn stepped back. "You're beautiful. Maybe one of those rich philanthro-pists will ask you out."

"I feel like we're playing dress-up. And…" She patted the Mustang. "Our coach will turn into a pumpkin."

Jessalyn forced a grin. "Come on, or we'll be late." She'd thought the same thing about her life with Theo. Whatever her midnight might be, it would strike, and Theo would pop out of her life.

They got in the car, and Jessalyn entered the address in the onboard GPS. "Have you figured out what you're going to say to people?"

Sally laughed. "Sort of. I want them to know how hard it is for some students to pay for classes and work if they don't want student loans, but I don't want to come across as needy. Even though I am, and I would love it if they paid for my schooling."

"I've got plenty of stories for them. I'm glad I don't need it anymore. It's been a big load off my shoulders to not have to worry about food and housing."

"And to have Theo pay your tuition."

Jessalyn frowned at her friend. "We haven't discussed my tuition."

Sally snorted. "He bought you this brand new car when he wouldn't let you walk to the bus. You know he's going to pay for your tuition. I wish I had a guy who loved me like that."

"He…" She clamped her mouth shut. Maybe he did love her. Since the first time she stepped into his house, there was desire in his eyes. Now, there was something more. Sometimes, he'd come up behind her and wrap his arms around her. He'd kiss the side of her neck, then continued on to whatever he was doing. There was no expectation that it might lead to having sex, and it wasn't pretending for an audience. It was more that he couldn't resist showing he cared.

They'd been driving beside a brick wall for a block when the GPS voice said they'd reached their destination. Jessalyn turned into the driveway at the opening. The house was almost as big as Theo's family home. The school must pay deans a lot of money. Of course, he could have inherited it or it could be his wife's home.

She stopped behind a Rolls-Royce. Seriously? That guy

could afford to make a donation. The man exited his car, and she made note of his appearance to talk to him later. A valet directed the driver as the man headed for the wide granite stairs. Then the valet waved her forward. It seemed crazy to have valet parking at a house. The walk from where the cars were parked was half the distance than when she parked at the mall.

She stopped beside the valet, and he opened her door. "Good evening, ladies." He handed her a small ticket with a number. She stuffed it in her purse. He glanced at Sally. "Hold on, and I'll assist you also."

He offered his hand, and Jessalyn took it. It was more difficult getting out of a car with a long dress. Once she stood, he released her hand and hurried to the other side and opened Sally's door. Jessalyn followed and couldn't help smiling at her friend's big grin.

He closed the door. "Have a good evening, ladies."

Sally watched until he drove the car away. "That guy has muscles on muscles. He must spend half his time working out."

Jessalyn drew in a long breath. Theo had lots of money, and he was a regular person. Most of these people probably weren't scary either. They knew they'd be donating money to a good cause. Her job was to show them how important it was so that they might give more.

Inside the door, a man stood at an elegant podium tucked into an alcove. "Names?"

"Sally Baker."

The man made a check mark on his paper and looked at Jessalyn.

Jessalyn A—"

"Waters. Here we go." He checked it off.

She hadn't gotten around to changing her name at school yet. She hadn't thought much about it, but also, she felt like she'd wake up from a dream and find out she wasn't married to Theo.

He pointed behind him. "If you two could put your purses in the lockers and take the key, you're all set."

The lockers were a dark wood, and except for some still having keys with different colors of twisty plastic cords attached, it appeared to be an ordinary cabinet. She'd never attended an event like this, but she hadn't expected to stow her purse. She shrugged and picked a locker with a dark green cord attached then shoved her purse inside."

The man motioned toward the key. "You can put that around your wrist. Now you're hands-free."

He scribbled on his paper, as if dismissing them.

She raised her eyebrows to Sally, who lifted her empty hands, a yellow cord and key hanging from her wrist. "Let's go meet some money bags."

"Sally!" Jessalyn jabbed an elbow at Sally's ribs, but she stepped out of reach.

Jessalyn caught up and they entered a large room together. A chandelier hung from the ceiling surrounded by many canister lights. A low dais was straight ahead with a podium in the center, and along another wall, a cloth covered table held trays of appetizers. No tables for dining were present. It was a good thing Theo had urged her to eat a snack before going.

About a dozen men in expensive suits, not tuxes, stood in groups. They ranged in age from thirty to sixty, but all the women seemed to be near her age. Two men carried trays with various size glasses on them, offering drinks to the attendees.

Sally stepped closer. "Hey, there's Angie. And I recognize a couple of the other girls from campus."

Jessalyn scanned the women's faces, not recognizing all of them. She'd seen some in her larger classes, but didn't remember their names. "And there's Whitley to the left, talking to that older guy." They seemed to be in an intense conversation—which was what they were there for. "Should we stick together or split up?"

"Mmm. Split up. We can cover more people that way."

With the number of students present, the philanthropists would be well covered.

"Okay. Let's compare notes in a bit." Jessalyn headed toward two men, one who had arrived in the Rolls. She stopped beside them and waited until the one talking finished. "Hi. I'm Jessalyn. I'm a nursing student."

The older, Rolls man on her left nodded. "I'm Terell."

The other man responded in a deep, rich voice. "I'm John."

"I'm so glad you're considering sponsoring students in the nursing program. I know how hard it is to have to work and take a smaller class load to pay for everything."

"You don't have student loans?" John asked.

She shook her head. "I didn't want to graduate with a lot of debt."

He frowned. "You could have finished sooner and used your larger salary to pay off the loan."

She shrugged. "I've got about a year-and-a-half left, and I'm fine with that. But I know of a couple students who couldn't handle both work and school and had to quit. Those are the ones who would benefit from this scholarship program."

"How do we find those students, and not ones who only want a free ride?"

"Maybe some funding can be offered after a student has completed a semester. A teacher or counselor who knows about their work situation can give them an application. Of course, that leaves out the people who want to become nursing students, but know they can't afford it. Maybe high school counselors can help by handing out applications. But that's probably the same for most need based scholarships."

"Jessalyn, thanks for offering your insight," John said.

That was a brush off if she ever heard one. "Have a nice evening, gentlemen." She headed toward the food table, wanting to get something into her stomach so it wouldn't growl at an awkward time.

"She's well spoken," Terell said before she got out of ear-shot.

A man, younger than the first two, stood beside the table, surveying the group. He was attractive, but with cold eyes. Maybe he didn't know anyone there.

She picked up a plate and a couple hors d'oeuvres, then ate one in two bites. She looked over the group, noticing for the first time that the only women present were the students. She'd never attended a wealthy fundraiser, but it seemed odd.

She stepped closer to the man. Maybe it was his first time at one of these things, too. He eyed her up and down with his eyes of stone.

"Hi. I'm Jessalyn."

"Jace."

He sure didn't seem like someone who would donate a lot of money to scholarships. Maybe he accompanied someone, except he'd probably have stuck with that person.

"I'm a nursing student."

"I might pay big bucks for a nurse." His gaze dropped to her chest. "You know anatomy?"

She didn't think he meant heal-a-patient kind of anatomy. No one had looked at her so blatantly before, and it made her skin crawl. "Yes. Um. I have to go talk to my friend." Appetite lost, she set her plate on a side table and stepped far enough away from him to regain some of her composure as she searched for Sally.

She overheard a voice behind that made her freeze. "You missed orientation."

What kind of fundraiser needed orientation?

Jace said, "I've been to these before. I don't need orientation."

"Obviously, you do." The man's voice showed irritation.

"Notice how this one is different?"

There was a long pause as if Jace were figuring it out. "Yeah. The girls are older than his usual selection and more relaxed. What'd you give them?"

The voice lowered to the point she had to strain to hear. "Nothing. They were told possible donors had to be convinced to give money to nursing scholarships."

"George outdid himself. Easier to pick which girls to take…"

Take. Jessalyn's heart pounded as she strolled with a sedate pace so as not to alert anyone she'd heard something she shouldn't. Her hands shook so she balled them into fists. She hoped her face didn't show her panic. She headed to where she thought restrooms would be. She couldn't be sick. She needed to get help. She'd trusted her professor about this evening. Was he in on it or had he been tricked, too?

A discreet restroom sign pointed down a hall. The first door opened to a single. Not too surprising for being in a house. She locked the door and pulled out her phone. All their purses had been taken, and she'd given in without a thought. It was only a lucky coincidence that she'd found the small pocket in her gown. She'd have to send texts so no one would overhear her talking. She sent a series of short messages to make sure something reached Theo. She couldn't chance that someone might stop her before hitting send on a long message.

Chapter 14

Theo read a book in his sitting room, not wanting to be with the family. He might have been seeing words, but it wasn't sinking in. He tossed the book down. This should be like any evening when Jessa worked at Zentaro's, but after she'd switched jobs a week ago, he'd gotten used to her being home in the evenings. Before Jessalyn, there were all kinds of things he did after dinner, but nothing held his interest.

He went to the cabinet in the corner and pulled out a glass and bottle of scotch. He poured a finger and strode to the window, staring out over the glass roofed pool. It was lit only by the security light near the door. He'd never look at the hot tub the same again after being in it with Jessa a few nights ago. Everyone had gone to their rooms, but he'd locked the door, just in case. After relaxing for a while, she'd straddled his lap and kissed him. No way had he let that invitation go by. He'd stripped them and sat her on the edge of the tub. Making love to her while they were hot and slick had been incredible.

His phone chimed with a text. He set down his glass and picked up the device.

Jessa. *Help*

He grinned. She must be bored to tears. He started to type when another message popped up.

They took our purses.

A chill invaded his heart and twisted. He dropped into his

chair and typed. *What?* Before he hit *Send*, another message came in.

Some George arranged this evening.
They're selling us.

"No!" Theo leaped up, stuffed his feet into his shoes, and raced out the door, heading to Susan and Gary's wing.

Another message chimed. *Someone's at the door. I love you.*

Jessa loved him, and Theo didn't have time to savor it. He erased his message, then sent a new one. *We're coming for you. I love you.*

He pounded on Susan and Gary's door. When it didn't open immediately, he pounded some more and twisted the doorknob, but it was locked. "Gary! I need your help!"

Gary opened the door while buttoning his shirt. "What's got *you* so upset?"

"It's Jessalyn. George has her and the other students." He held his phone out.

"What?" Gary snatched the phone and read Jessa's texts. "Where is she?"

"I don't know! The address was on the invitation, but I didn't pay attention to it, and she took it with her." He should have noticed it. With the threats against her, he should have realized the deception. They had to find her. He didn't know what he'd do if they couldn't.

"Show me her number." Gary pulled out his phone and dialed. "Beck. It's Gary. I need to track a phone number location ASAP." He recited it from Theo's phone. "Possible kidnapping and trafficking."

At least Theo didn't have to waste time explaining the whole situation to Gary. The police detective understood the threat.

Every second counted to get Jessa back. At any moment, she could be whisked off to anywhere. Even out of the country. She'd be raped and beaten. He couldn't let that happen to her, but he was helpless to do anything unless they found her.

He should have insisted on going with her. He gave money to charities, and if this fundraiser had been a legitimate charity, he and his money would have been welcome.

Gary stuck his head back in the door. "I've got to go out. Jessalyn's been taken." He raced down the stairs, phone to his ear, with Theo on his heels.

"Thanks." Gary stopped, held the phone between his head and shoulder, and scribbled in his notebook. "Put me through to Luke." He ran out the front door, and Theo followed.

Gary explained the situation to Luke. "Okay, tell them no sirens and to park in the street at least a hundred feet from the driveway." He raised his voice. "And detain anybody who leaves that property!"

They got into the car. Gary switched the phone to his other ear and started the engine. "Sorry. I'm worried about my sister-in-law. See you when we get there." Gary stuck his phone in his shirt pocket and backed out of the driveway. He gave Theo a quick glance. "Mansard's finished. Whatever he's up to, he's done tonight."

"I don't care as long as Jessa is safely returned." Theo tied the shoes he'd hastily donned.

The twenty minutes to their destination, Theo's stomach knotted up tighter and tighter. Jessa could be hurt or gone by the time they got there. They couldn't be too late. His last text might be the only time he told her 'I love you'. If...No, *when* they got her back, he'd tell her and show her every day how much he loved her. He bounced his feet on the floor, anxious to jump into action.

Gary had hit his emergency lights a couple of times to get slow moving vehicles out of the way. His hands gripped the wheel so tight his knuckles were white.

They traveled beside a seven foot brick wall for almost a block then Gary parked on the side of the road behind a darkened police cruiser. A uniformed officer stood with his arms crossed, leaning against the car. Beside a black SUV, two men appeared to be having a heated discussion in low voices. They stood about twenty feet from an entrance in the wall. Two more SUVs were parked on the opposite side of the road, but down the other way from the opening.

"That doesn't look good," Gary said.

Theo's heart stopped. They couldn't be too late. He had to get Jessalyn back. "What?"

Gary cracked his door open. "Luke is talking with someone I don't recognize, and two of those SUVs aren't ours."

All three of the vehicles looked the same to Theo. Maybe the man was someone who came out of the mansion. Except, he would have been handcuffed and arrested.

Theo was a step behind Gary as they joined the men. One was in jeans and a sweatshirt. The other wore a suit.

The man in jeans glanced toward them and pointed at Theo. "That man's wife is in there. I'm not waiting and taking chances with her life or the other women's." He must be Luke since he knew Jessalyn's situation.

The other man leaned in. If he was going for intimidation, it wasn't working. "We've surveilled Mansard for six months, and we're not stepping in there one second before the planned time."

Theo didn't want to wait. He couldn't. Jessa needed saving now before anything else happened to her.

Gary cleared his throat. "Luke, what's going on?"

The man in jeans waved toward the other man. "Meet FBI Special Agent Cameron Ellis. Man in *charge*," he said with a sneer, and shook his head. "Sorry, Theo. My hands are tied. I was forced to send away most of my men."

Theo had figured that as soon as they arrived, a group of police officers would storm the doors, and very soon, he'd have Jessa in his arms. Now, they were on FBI time, and it could be hours, with who-knows-what happening to her.

Ellis slipped a hand in his jacket pocket. "I've got a man

inside, and he says everything's fine. They're doing the auction now. The girls don't know what's going on."

"Except for Jessalyn." Theo brought up the texts and turned the screen toward Ellis.

The man frowned. "Let's hope she doesn't give herself away."

Theo's breath caught in his throat. "And if she does?"

Ellis patted Theo's shoulder. "She'll be fine. It's almost over."

The hollow words offered no reassurance. All that seemed important to the agent was completing his mission as planned, and it didn't matter if a few women got damaged in the process. Theo put his hands on his head, anger mounting at the situation, and his stomach twisted more than on the way over. He felt totally helpless.

~~~

Jessalyn deleted each message in case someone found her phone. She didn't want anyone discovering that help was on the way. The hardest to delete was the one where Theo said he loved her for the first time.

She stuffed her phone in her hidden pocket, ran water in the sink for a few seconds, then opened the door. A man stood outside, and she clamped her lips tight together so she wouldn't scream. He didn't need to know she was on edge or he'd wonder why. She side-stepped to get around him, but he grasped her arm. She froze, forcing herself to stay still and not yank her arm away.

He stared down at her from a height taller than Theo. "You were in there a long time. Are you all right?" As if he cared.

"One of the appetizers didn't agree with me, but I'm all right now." She gazed into his eyes, daring him to disbelieve her. She probably appeared pale from her fear, which could be taken as illness. In any normal situation, she wouldn't be questioned about her time spent in the bathroom, which emphasized even more that this was not a charitable event.

Something flickered in his eyes, and she would have thought it was sympathy, except he was there to buy women. He nodded and released her. "You should probably avoid any more food or drink."

"Good idea." Jessalyn wondered why he would offer advice. She made her way back to the ballroom on shaky legs. The man who'd checked them in stood beside the entry door, arms behind his back—like a soldier at ease. Nobody would get past him unless they were supposed to.

She hoped a lot of police would come in all at once, but she couldn't count on anyone getting there in time.

Sally stood with three men and waved her hands as she talked to them. Even if she'd noticed sooner that none of the men appeared to have dates, it would have been too late anyway. They weren't leaving here on their own.

She had to pretend nothing was wrong. It wouldn't do any good to scare the other women, and would probably make things worse for all of them. If they screamed and ran for the exit, someone might get beaten or shot. And Jessalyn would be in the worst position for inciting a riot.

Jessalyn couldn't continue talking to the men about how great scholarships would be, knowing full well they weren't interested. They wanted to stare at her body and hear her talk. She joined Sally, who finished telling her personal story before glancing at her. The men, on the other hand, ogled her as if she were fresh meat. She'd become a commodity.

"What's your story?" the man standing beside her asked.

No need to urge them for a scholarship donation, but she'd have to say something. "I've been working my way through nursing school, paying as I go."

"Commendable. I like hard workers."

At the beginning of the evening, she wouldn't have thought anything of his comment. Now, her mind bounced in several directions at once. She'd have the backbone to have sex, hour after hour, day after day. Maybe she'd be bought for an actual slave—sex and housekeeping. Or maybe she'd become part of a harem. She'd read somewhere that men who lived in eastern countries loved blondes. Or maybe some of them wanted a nurse they only had to pay for once.

A raised voice behind her had everybody turning to face the podium. "Good evening, ladies and gentlemen. We're beginning the auction part of our event."

She hadn't talked to this man, but had seen him talking to various men. If she didn't know better, she'd think he was a nice guy.

The auctioneer gestured to his left at a table with various items lined up on it. "I'm sure you've had a chance to inspect all the items we're auctioning this evening."

She hadn't seen them, but it didn't matter. Those items weren't on the auction block.

"I'm going to have our lovely nursing students help with this part. Ladies, when your name is called, I'd like you to pick up the next auction item, display it in front of the crowd,"—He swept his arm, showing the path they should take—"then come up here beside me."

Giving the men a last time to ogle each of them up close before bidding started. It was disgusting.

A man standing beside the table had a clipboard in hand. He read off, "Patricia."

A woman she knew by sight approached the table, and clipboard guy pointed at the first item. She picked up a vase of glass flowers and cruised across the front of the dais, a smile on her face.

Once Patricia stood beside the auctioneer, he spoke. "Let's start bidding at a thousand dollars."

The girl's eyebrows popped up. In a normal situation, the flowers would be sold long before reaching this starting bid. But for people? Jessalyn had no idea what the going rate was. After a quick back and forth between two men, the highest bid was eleven thousand dollars.

"Thank you, Patricia." The auctioneer pointed to a table behind him. "You can put those there."

Patricia set down her flowers and joined one of the other women, not realizing that she'd lost her freedom for several thousand dollars.

Clipboard guy finished writing on his paper, then called out. "Angie."

The woman was a beautiful little elf with auburn hair. She barely came to Jessalyn's chin, but was a dynamo of energy. She hurried to the table and clipboard guy pointed to the next item. She picked up a painting of a forest scene with a river, maybe twelve by eighteen inches. Angie held it over her head and made a slow spin, then waltzed along beside the dais, still holding it high. Once she stood beside podium guy, she lowered it to chest level.

He grinned. "Shall we begin with a thousand?"

Four hands shot up. The thousands escalated quickly, finally going to Jace for twenty-seven thousand. Jessalyn shivered. She wouldn't want to be owned by a guy with that cold stare. But would any of the men be better?

It suddenly clicked that she'd been through this before, the aftereffects, anyway. She'd been sold, but it was nothing like this. Theo had stepped in because he didn't want her to be hurt. And here she was, about to be sold to someone, again because of George Mansard. This outcome would be similar to what would have happened to her without Theo. She'd disappear. They all would. Sally's mother would never see Sally again. So many family and friends would be hurt, too, because of these men.

She couldn't ask for a man more loving and understanding

than Theo. She imagined her disappearing into the slave trade would destroy him worse than if she died.

"Whitley." Clipboard guy's voice brought her back to the scene. The beautiful Puerto Rican woman stepped forward and picked up a black stone sculpture of a man on a horse. Whitley carried it closer to her body as if it was heavy. Once she stepped onto the dais, she set the figure on the table.

Jace had the winning bid again. Then Theresa was called, and was bought by a different man.

"Jessalyn."

Her heart pounded, and she gulped down bile. She had to pretend she didn't know what the bidding was actually for. A bit of trembling might be interpreted as fear of being in front of a crowd, but she'd rather show strength before these men.

Clipboard guy pointed at an eighteen inch tall brass statue of a scantily clad belly dancer. It figured that she'd get the half naked one. She picked it up by the neck and ankles and strode along the front of the dais. She hadn't paid much attention to the men as the other women paraded past. Now, she wished she hadn't noticed the men's creepy leers. She had a feeling that, whatever they planned for all of the women, they'd do a *test drive* first.

She climbed the steps and stood beside the auctioneer.

"Starting bid—"

The man she'd run into outside the bathroom lifted a hand. "Two thousand."

Was it weird that she hoped she'd be sold for a lot of money, even though she didn't want to be sold? If someone paid a lot, they'd want their investment to last. She hoped.

No one would pay as much as Theo had paid to save her.

Two other hands shot up, the men calling out bids. It was a three-way war until the bid hit twenty thousand, then the first man dropped out. Again, she thought she caught sympathy in his eyes.

She glanced down at the statue in her hands, catching a glint on her engagement ring. If any of the men had noticed it, they'd probably realized they could get part of their money back from buying her by selling her rings. Theo had paid nearly fifteen thousand for them. If she wasn't rescued in time, she'd lose her only connection to him.

She startled when the auctioneer called out.

"Sold for forty-two thousand."

She hadn't paid attention to who'd won the bid. She set the statue on the table and joined Sally. It wouldn't be long before it was her turn to be sold.

As the rest of the auction flew by, Jessalyn's thoughts were on Theo. It was almost over, and no rescuer had arrived.

The auctioneer raised his arms. "This auction is successfully concluded. Bring on the champagne."

Two waiters came out with trays. The women had bunched together and were served from one tray and the men from another. As Jessalyn picked up a glass, she wondered if it was drugged. It would be the easiest way to get them out of there.

The auctioneer lifted his glass. "Thank you, ladies, for joining us tonight and making this evening a success."

Everyone drank from their glasses. Where was a plant when she needed one? Jessalyn put her glass to her lips, but didn't drink. She lowered the glass a few inches, bringing it close to her chest and dumped its contents into her dress. Hopefully her bra would absorb the liquid. Or maybe not. A trickle of liquid slipped past her bra and darkened the fabric below it.

Sally whispered. "I can't believe how much all this stuff sold for. It's going to make a huge difference for some of the students."

A huge difference for *these* students. Jessalyn grabbed Sally's arm and leaned close. "Look, Sally, I think…"

Her friend swayed, eyes glazed over. A glass shattered on the floor and one of the women collapsed, followed by another.

Sally's eyes closed. "I don't feel…" She fell to the floor.

Two other women were still standing. Jessalyn didn't want to be a suspicious last, so she closed her eyes and dropped down beside Sally, lying face down so the wet would be hidden. She hoped that once she was carried outside, she could take the man by surprise and escape.

Chapter 15

Theo couldn't stand around waiting while someone might be raping Jessa. He needed to get to her. He walked along the brick wall, clenching and unclenching his hands. At about fifty feet from the gate, he glanced toward the FBI agents, still busy in their discussions. Ignoring Gary, a few feet behind, he leaped and grabbed the top of the wall. He scrabbled for footholds on the brick and threw a leg over the top. Pain lanced his thigh, and he held back a groan. The top of the wall was studded with one-inch spikes. When he'd positioned his hands, he'd been lucky. Not so much for his leg.

The whine of a helicopter starting drew his attention. A man in a suit shuffled toward it, carrying a woman over his shoulder. Theo's gut tightened. She wore a dress the same color as Jessa's. Then he caught sight of the woman's blonde hair. It was her. *No!* His chest squeezed so tight he couldn't breathe. No one was taking Jessa, if he could help it.

He threw his other leg over the wall, avoiding putting it on a spike, but adding more pressure on the first leg. Pain, he could live with, but he couldn't live without Jessa. He leaped off the wall, landing on his feet, knees bent. Theo sprinted across the lawn as if he was doing a fifty-yard dash, and the finish line was Jessa. No competition had ever been more important than this. In a dozen steps she'd disappear into the chopper and be gone forever.

A muffled gunshot behind him only spurred him faster.

Jessa was all that mattered.

Jessa screamed, "Help! Help me!" And she started struggling, distracting the man from Theo's approach. She pounded on his back, and the guy stopped, whacking her on the butt. Theo rammed his shoulder into the brute's ribs, and Jessa shrieked as she was thrown, landing about five feet away.

Theo took the man down and pummeled his face. Another man jumped out of the chopper and ran toward Jessa. *No!* As Theo started to pull away, the guy beneath him grabbed Theo's arm and hit him in the jaw, whipping his head to the side. The runner drew closer to Jessa, and Theo tugged to get free. A red blob bloomed on the runner's shoulder, and he fell to the ground. Theo peered behind.

Gary pointed his gun toward the helicopter and yelled out. "This is the police! Turn the chopper off and get out here."

The man beneath Theo hit him again. Luckily this time, it was only a glancing blow. At the same moment the engine powered down, Theo punched the man hard enough his hand ached, but it seemed to knock the guy out.

A man in jeans and T-shirt jumped out of the helicopter, hands above his head. "I was hired for the day. I don't know what's going on here."

Gary jumped out behind him, his gun never wavering. "On the ground, face down." Theo had only seen him this serious when he was protecting Susan.

The pilot dropped to the ground.

"FBI. Hands up," a new voice yelled.

Theo looked toward the speaker in the FBI jacket and the gun pointing at him. This agent hadn't been one of the men Luke had talked to. Theo got off the guy he'd beaten and lifted his hands.

Gary lowered his gun and stepped closer to Theo, eying the newcomer. "I'm police detective Gary Wassman. Special Agent Ellis knows I'm here. Well, on site." He nodded toward

Theo. "He's my...wife's stepson." He nodded toward Jessa, who was getting to her feet. "And she's his wife."

The agent lowered his gun and glanced toward Jessalyn.

Theo didn't think a woman could run fast in heels on grass, but Jessa proved him wrong. His throat tightened. She was safe. Her body hit his hard, forcing the air from his lungs. Reflex brought his arms down, and they clung to each other. He kissed her temple and blinked as his eyes stung. Nothing would ever feel as good as having her in his arms.

Ten more feet and she would have been gone. If he'd been seconds later, both their lives would have been destroyed. He held her tighter, his whole body trembling. It would be a long time before he'd let her out of his sight.

The agent pointed toward the men on the ground. "I'll take care of them." He strode toward the trio.

Theo lifted Jessa's chin, and stared into her beautiful, tear-streaked face. "I love you." His heart soared being able to say it directly to her.

She gave him a wobbly grin. "I love you, too. Thank you for rescuing me. Again."

"I'll always be here to rescue you. I'm kind of selfish that way because I can't live without you."

She laid her head on his chest, then her whole body stiffened.

"Hey, what's wrong?"

She lifted her head. "That man who's coming out of the building was one of the bidders."

The man wore a well tailored suit and stopped to talk to one of the agents then glanced in their direction. He must be the agent they had inside, but Jessa wouldn't know that. He said a few more words to the man who seemed to be in charge and started toward Theo, Jessa, and Gary. Jessa pushed into Theo.

The well dressed man stopped beside them. "I'm Special Agent Lance Cross." Jessa's body relaxed. "Glad to see your guy rescued you. I was dealing with the arrests, and when I turned around, you'd already been taken." He narrowed his eyes. "I'm guessing you took my advice to not eat or drink anything more since you're the only conscious woman."

She pulled away from Theo, her cheeks a nice shade of pink. "I dumped the champagne into my dress so they wouldn't know I hadn't drunk it." She rubbed Theo's shirt. Sure enough, his shirt was saturated.

Agent Cross grinned. "And I hear you figured out the situation and texted your guy about it. Staying cool and smart under pressure are good characteristics for a nurse. Or an FBI agent. You might consider it." He tipped his head and joined the man in charge.

Theo kissed her. "He's right. You sending me that text brought me here so I had the chance to rescue you." His eyes burned again. It might take a long time to get over the thought of how close he'd come to losing her. "You saved yourself every bit as much as I saved you."

One of the FBI agents Theo had seen out front stopped to talk to the agent in charge then approached them. "Jessalyn Waters?"

She glanced at Theo. "It's actually Jessalyn Argyle. I haven't changed my school records yet."

"Yes, ma'am. I'm Agent Ethan Sheldon. I need to ask you a few questions."

She turned to face the Sheldon fully, her back flush to Theo. He wrapped his arms around her waist, giving her his support.

The agent lifted a small tablet. "Let's start with how you came to be here."

She stiffened, and Theo pulled her closer. "One of my professors invited us. He gave us printed invitations."

Agent Sheldon frowned. "Which one?"

"Professor Donovan. Kevin Donovan."

The agent tapped his ear and angled his body away from

them. "Katie? Send someone to question Professor Kevin Donovan...Yeah, he handed out invitations to the women...Thanks." He turned back to them. "He's getting picked up. Now, tell me what happened, starting when you entered the house.

Theo's blood ran cold at Jessa's description of the event. Gary's stiff stance and tight mouth showed he wasn't handling it any better. He was probably reliving rescuing Susan and bringing her back from the brink of death.

Jessa reached the part where she had texted him when Agent Sheldon interrupted.

"How did you have your phone if you'd given up your purse?"

She pulled her phone from the hidden pocket in her dress. "It's probably for a lipstick, but my phone fit. Barely."

Theo had tried to get her to buy a better cell phone, but she'd resisted. Now he was glad she had. A new one wouldn't have fit in her pocket. It was amazing how her life had hinged on her owning old, outdated technology. So many things had worked together to keep her alive and safe.

She finished with how Theo had come out of nowhere while she struggled to get out of the buyer's hold.

The agent's gaze switched to Theo. "And how did you get in here?"

Theo thumbed over his shoulder. "I climbed that wall."

The man's eyebrows shot up. "The wall with spikes on top? Didn't you see the warning signs?"

"No, but I wouldn't let a few scratches stop be from getting to Jessalyn."

Gary stepped back. "You mean the scratches that are soaking your pants with blood?"

"What?" Jessa pushed Theo's arms away and grabbed his bicep, turning him. "Theo! You could have bled to death."

Now that attention was drawn to his injury, the pain came roaring back, but he was sure the bleeding couldn't be that bad.

"Paramedics are out front taking care of the women." Agent Sheldon thumbed over his shoulder. "You might want to have them see to that." He added more data to his tablet. "I've got your information. We'll contact you again tomorrow with anything else." He walked away.

Jessa tugged Theo's arm. "Let's get your leg taken care of."

Theo glanced at Gary. "How did you get over the wall without a scratch?"

Gary pointed behind him. "I blew the lock on the door in the wall and came through that."

Theo nodded. "That's what I heard. I was sure I'd get shot in the back." And he hadn't cared as long as he could stop that man from taking Jessa. "Maybe I should have—"

Gary shook his head. "I came through after you'd already taken that guy down. He'd have been on the chopper with Jessalyn before we made it through the door." He squeezed Theo's shoulder. "In my opinion, it was well worth the injury."

Theo hugged Jessa. He agreed totally. If the cut got infected and his leg had to be amputated, he'd consider it a worthy exchange for her freedom and safety.

He followed her into the building, passing through a huge room where a row of men lay on the floor with their hands cuffed behind their backs—two of them being the men he and Gary had taken care of. The other one was probably in an ambulance. Two men stood over them. Four women, still unconscious, were on the floor with blankets draped over them. Theo pulled Jessa closer, his eyes stinging again.

They passed out the front door and into blue and red flashing lights. People stood in several groups. Jessa marched him to the nearest ambulance. A paramedic strapped a blood pressure cuff on an unconscious woman wearing an oxygen mask. That could have been Jessa if she hadn't been so observant. She could be unconscious, getting farther away on that helicopter. He pulled her into a tight hug. No. She was here—

safe.

After the paramedic finished, Jessa spoke up. "Can you help us?"

He turned around.

"My husband got cut rescuing me. Can you check his leg?"

It delighted Theo that she was worried about him. It was the first time he'd heard her call him her husband, and he liked it.

The paramedic frowned at her. "Are you one of the women? I should check you first."

She shook her head. "I didn't drink the drug, so I'm fine." She tugged Theo closer. "But my husband got cut on spikes in the wall. Theo, turn."

The paramedic inhaled a quick breath. "Do you mind if I cut your pant leg off?"

"They're ruined anyway. Go for it."

The man gripped Theo's pant leg and sliced up then around. The cold steel touched his leg. "Jeez, man. You did a number on yourself. You really need stitches."

"I'm not going to the hospital. I'm taking my wife home, so do the best you can."

Jessa tried to step behind him, but he held her tight. He didn't want her to see it while he was a bloody mess. The sting sharpened, and he glanced over his shoulder. The medic was spraying a stream of liquid on the cut. He sucked in a breath and flinched. His hands tightened on Jessa for a second before he loosened his grip. She'd had enough trauma for one night. She didn't need bruises he caused.

The medic dried the injury. "I'm putting on a bunch of Steri-Strips, but you really should get stitches tonight. You can take a quick shower with them, but no soaking. Pat them dry. They should stay on about a week before falling off." He taped on some gauze and stood up. He stuffed a handful of packaged gauze pads, his roll of tape, and a tube of antibiotic ointment into a bag and held them out. "Here. Change it twice a day."

"Thanks." Jessa took the bag, holding it against her body. "Wait!" She grabbed the paramedic's arm. "How are the other women?"

"They're all stable. We're keeping them overnight for observation."

"So the drug isn't going to cause any permanent damage?"

He shook his head. "Doesn't look that way. Breathing and heart rate are fine. Pupils are responsive. But the hospital staff will keep a close watch on them just to be sure."

"Thank you. I'm glad they're going to be okay."

She held her arm up with a key dangling from her wrist. "I want to go back in for my purse." She led him inside and into an alcove, then yanked off the key. She studied the key then stuck it into a lock in the wall. A small door opened, and she snatched up her purse, juggled it with the medical items, which Theo took from her, then she grasped his hand.

"Let's get out of here," Theo said. They went outside, and he scanned the crowd for Gary, finding him with the agent in charge. "Gary!"

Gary joined them.

"We're going home in Jessalyn's car. All the women's purses are in the lockers near the door. They're wearing the keys on their wrists." He wrapped an arm around Jessa.

Chapter 16

Jessalyn was exhausted. The hours of fear had taken a toll. They'd stopped by Sally's house to tell her mom what had happened and where Sally was. The little she'd told the woman was enough to make Jessalyn cry again.

She was glad Theo had driven. She was too shaken. He'd grimaced a couple times when he pushed in the clutch, and she offered to drive, but he refused.

After he drove the car into the garage, getting out was more than she could handle. He came around, helped her from her seat, and surrounded her with his arms. Safe. She should have been all cried out, but the tears flowed again.

He hugged her tighter. "Shh. Shh. You're safe. He can't hurt you now."

A tear rolled down his cheek, and she wiped it away.

Theo kissed her fingers. "I thought I'd lost you. I thought they'd done despicable things to you. You were level-headed enough to text me, and that's what saved you. The FBI would have let you slip between their fingers." Another tear tracked down his cheek.

She pulled his head down and kissed him. "We both saved me. I want to go inside and snuggle into your arms all night so I know I'm safe."

"That's exactly what we both need." Theo closed the car door, and with his arm still around her, they entered the house.

Susan sat at the kitchen table with a cup between her

hands. She ran across the room and hugged both of them. "Gary called me." She squeezed Jessalyn's shoulder. "I am so sorry you suffered through this." She looked at Theo. "Gary said you're a hero, stopping them from taking Jessalyn on a helicopter."

Jessalyn didn't want to relive this night, but it scrolled through her head. She shivered, and Theo tightened his arm around her. It had been too close. Seconds, too close.

Someone had shouted "FBI", and a big guy had snatched her off the floor, tossing her over his shoulder. She should have screamed as soon as he picked her up, but her brain was in follow-the-plan mode, and that was to wait until they got outside.

She hadn't seen the helicopter but knew what it was when it started. She'd be thrown on board and never see Theo again. She'd screamed and tried to wiggle off the guy's shoulder, slamming her fists into his back, but he'd been too strong.

No more. She was home now.

Theo glanced down at her and pulled her closer. "Thanks, Susan. We'll see you in the morning."

He scooped her into his arms, and kissed her forehead. Nothing like the way that other man had manhandled her. She wrapped an arm around the back of his neck, and he carried her up the stairs and into their room, setting her on the bed. She was safe, in familiar surroundings that she'd grown to love almost as much as the man who'd rescued her.

Jessalyn drew in a long breath, then another. It was over. The bad guys were arrested.

She stood up and hugged Theo. "I love you."

He squeezed her. "I love you so much."

She'd had to delete the first time he'd said it to her. She extracted her life-saving phone from her pocket. "Can you do something for me?"

"Anything. I would give my life for you."

She knew he meant it. "I erased our texts so if someone

140

took my phone, they wouldn't know help was on the way. Can you send me *I love you* again?"

He grinned and pulled out his phone. He typed a while before her phone vibrated with a new message.

She picked it up and checked his name. *I love you. I love you more than life. I love you forever. I love you beyond forever.*

Jessalyn's chest constricted and tears stung her eyes. Tonight, she might have lost him forever, but they'd fought hard for each other. She set her phone down and kissed him. "I'm never deleting that message." She leaned back to see his face. "If we weren't already married, I'd ask *you* to marry me. I love you so much."

He closed his eyes and let out a long breath. "When I told you we were getting married, I thought you'd hate me forever."

"I was resentful, but I never hated you. When Mitch was driving me over here, I imagined you'd put me in a locked room in the basement and only visit me when you, um, needed physical release."

His eyes widened, then he chuckled. "I need you for more than that. I'm not going to ask for forgiveness for making Mitch bring you to my house, because I still stand by that. But please forgive me for being a jerk and forcing you to sleep in my bed."

She stared at him, never expecting any kind of concession on that. She'd grown comfortable in his house and with him faster because he had, but she wouldn't tell him that.

He froze, his gaze on her face. The sparkle left his eyes. "You can't forgive me?"

She drew in a long breath. "Well, you were a jerk." Jessalyn didn't think she'd seen him pout before. She almost grinned, but held it in. "But a gentleman, too. And you rescued me twice." She placed her hands on his cheeks. "And I can't imagine loving anyone the way I love you. So, I forgive you."

His shoulders dropped, and he lifted her up, kissing her and laughing. "Thank you."

The weight of the day smacked her, and she sagged.

"Hey, let's get you to bed." He turned her and unzipped her dress.

"I need to throw this dress away. I don't want to ever see it again." The dress had cost a fortune, but she'd have nightmares every time she looked at it.

He slid the gown down her body. "I'll get it dry cleaned and donate it to an organization that provides prom dresses for underprivileged girls."

She narrowed her eyes. "How do you know about that kind of group?"

He glanced away and back at her. "An old girlfriend heads one up."

"Old girlfriend, huh?" She was surprised there was no sting in thinking about that.

"Yeah. Old, boring girlfriend."

She stepped out of the dress and Theo draped it over a chair. He removed the rest of her clothes and tucked her into bed, then stripped and joined her. His warm body twined with hers. She was exactly where she needed to be—in the loving arms of her husband.

As she drifted off to sleep, Jessalyn remembered the man sitting on the bench on campus, leering at her. She hoped he'd been arrested with Mansard.

~~~

Theo woke to Jessa's crying and pulled her tighter into his arms. "Shh. Baby, you're safe. I'm here. I won't let anything happen to you." He wished he'd seen through the invitation so she wouldn't have experienced the terror of being sold at auction.

She buried her face in his neck. "Theo, hold me tighter."

He hugged her more firmly, being careful not to hurt her.

"I've got you. I'm not letting go."

"I kept seeing that guy Jace. All the men leered, but that guy" —she shivered, and he rubbed her back— "had the coldest eyes. I-I dreamed about him telling me how he would torture me because I wouldn't…let him…" She burst into tears, deep wracking sobs.

"Baby, you're safe. You'll never see him again. He's going to prison for a really long time." Theo hoped the guy would get a life sentence.

Jessa sniffled. "I'm sorry. I—"

He ran his hand down the back of her head and kissed her forehead. "Shh. You have nothing to be sorry for. You have every right to be upset and scared."

He'd never been so terrified in his life. He kept rubbing her back and neck, needing the same reassurance she did.

She calmed and her body relaxed. Soon after, she fell asleep. He stayed awake longer, what-ifs playing in his head. He turned her so they spooned and buried his nose in her peach scented hair. Every breath reminded him that she was with him, safe. Moonlight slanted across the floor, only to be gradually obscured by a passing cloud. Finally, he drifted off to sleep.

~~~

"Mmm," Theo mumbled. It took a second for it to register that Jessa was kissing his chest and her hand massaged his butt. Already he throbbed hard against her stomach. There couldn't be a better way to wake up.

Early light barely lit the room. Theo had thought she'd sleep late. He didn't mind that she hadn't. At one point last evening, he thought he'd never see her again, that they'd never have this again. "Morning, baby."

She tipped her head up and grinned. "I thought you'd never wake up."

"Been at it a while?"

She kissed him. "Long enough."

He wiggled and thrust his pelvis forward. "If you touched me here, I might have woken up faster."

She giggled. "Maybe. But I kind of liked feeling it grow between us."

He kissed her nose and smiled. "Now that you've got its attention, and mine, what are you going to do about it?"

She nudged him onto his back and climbed on top of him. "How about this?"

"Seems perfect." He pointed to the nightstand drawer. "But you might want to get a condom before we get too far."

She bit her lip. "Um. I was thinking."

He ran his hands from her hips to her small waist and ribs then back down. "What were you thinking?"

"That if I took you up on your offer to pay for my schooling and I quit work just before school starts…"

He grinned, liking the sound of that. He could spend so much more time with her.

"And if I take full loads for spring and summer semesters, I'd be done. And that if I got pregnant now…"

His fingers tightened over her hips. He could imagine her getting large with their baby.

"The baby would be born soon after I graduate. I could take a break before job searching."

He took her hands and kissed her fingers. "I love you. I think that's the best idea since I a— told you we were getting married."

She leaned over and kissed him. "I love you, too."

He smiled. "You know, to make this work, you have to—"

She slapped a hand over his mouth. "I know."

He chuckled, but as soon as she held him in her hand and slid partway over him, he groaned. He'd never had such exquisite torture. She hovered, teasing him. He couldn't take it. He gripped her hips and surged upward. She dropped down with him, impaling herself to the hilt. He'd never thought that forgoing that bit of latex would make their coming together that much more special.

He lifted and lowered her, encouraging a steady rhythm. Then he caressed her breast, the smoothest skin he'd ever touched, and squeezed her nipple, drawing a moan from her as she tightened around him.

His intense need for her ensured he wouldn't last. Theo reached between them and touched her center, causing her to moan and tighten around him. She increased her pace, grinding down on his hand each time she dropped. After a few strokes, she shuddered, pulsing around him. He sat up partially and hugged her to his chest, letting her take him with her.

He fell back, and she followed. He didn't care if he ever breathed normally again. This woman could have his every breath. Their relationship may have started with the payment of money, but he'd also given her his heart, and he didn't regret it. As much as he enjoyed their lovemaking, everything about Jessa was important to him.

She lifted off him and looked down, grimacing. "Ew. That's messier than with condoms."

He laughed. "But not as fun." He sat up. "Come on. Let's go shower." By the time he finished helping her wash, he'd be ready for round two. They hadn't made love in the shower yet.

Chapter 17

Jessalyn entered the kitchen, holding hands with Theo. She couldn't let go. While getting dressed, she had to keep watching him, afraid he'd leave her alone. She'd checked the message on her phone from him and smiled before tucking it into her pocket. She didn't think she'd be able to go anywhere again without her phone.

Bradley jumped up. "Jessalyn." He hurried over and hugged her. "I'm glad you're all right."

"Me, too." She clasped Theo's hand tighter. "Turns out, Theo's the one who got injured." Her emotional injuries didn't show, but Theo had already helped, and no doubt would continue to.

Bradley clapped his hand on Theo's shoulder. "Hey, what happened to you?"

"My thigh got cut on some spikes on the top of a wall. No big deal."

Jessalyn glared at Theo. "They wanted him to go to the hospital for stitches, but settled for putting Steri-Strips on it." She'd changed the bandage after their shower. The deep laceration looked painful, but he acted like it was nothing.

Theo gave her a side hug and kissed her temple. "I have my own private nurse."

Autumn hugged her next, her expression adoring. "Mom said bad guys tried to take you, but Theo saved you."

146

Jessalyn was surprised they'd said anything to the young girl. "That's right. Theo's my hero."

Autumn glanced at Gary. "Gary's my hero. He helped me save Mom from a bad lady."

Jessalyn raised her eyebrows in Theo's direction.

He mouthed *Later.*

Jessalyn smiled at the girl. "Wow. Two heroes live here. I don't know if the house is big enough for both of them."

Autumn giggled. "They're not that big."

"Autumn, are you ready to swim now?" Susan stood.

"Yes!" The girl raced for the stairs.

Susan rubbed Jessalyn's arm. "Take it easy today."

Jessalyn lifted Theo's hand. "I'm not leaving the house. And I'm keeping Theo near me."

Susan glanced at Gary. "I know exactly what you mean. Well, I better catch up with my little fish."

Theo pulled out a chair for Jessalyn. "Why don't you sit down, and I'll dish up some food?"

"Okay." She was safe in the house. She knew that, but she couldn't be alone yet.

He set their plates on the table, sat beside her, and rubbed her thigh. He glanced at Jessalyn before turning to Gary. "What happened after we left?"

Gary set his cup down. "The FBI opened all the lockers and matched IDs with the women so they could notify families."

"Angie." Jessalyn ached for the woman. "She doesn't have family. She told me that she spent her teens in foster care." Jessalyn didn't know how she would have dealt with the aftereffects of the evening without Theo. Angie didn't even have a boyfriend.

"I called the hospital this morning," Gary said. "They all regained consciousness sometime during the night and will be released by lunchtime."

She blew out a long breath. "Good. I'll have to give Sally

and Angie calls later."

Theo took her hand. "What about Mansard? Was he arrested?"

"He wasn't onsite."

"No! He's still out there?" Fear rocketed back into her, leaving her heart pounding and hands shaking.

Theo wrapped an arm tightly around her.

Gary spread his hands. "No. They got him. The FBI planned to arrest Mansard at the same time as arrests at the fundraiser last night, so they couldn't warn the other."

Jessalyn's shoulders dropped. She was safe. Maybe. "They won't let him out on bail, will they?"

Gary shook his head. "No. With all his money, he's a flight risk. Most of the others will be held until trial, too."

"What about the man with the helicopter?" He'd paid for her. Maybe he'd try to find and kidnap her.

Gary chuckled. "Victor Cortez lives on a Caribbean island outside of U.S. jurisdiction. They won't be releasing him before his trial. He..." Gary closed his mouth and glanced at Theo, then dropped his gaze to his coffee.

Jessalyn leaned forward. "He what, Gary?"

"One of the FBI agents told me he's not a pimp, but he's got a harem which he sometimes shares. Nobody's ever escaped from his island."

That would have been her fate. "Are they going to rescue the women there?"

A pained expression crossed his face. "I hope so. But it's out of the country, so our authorities will have to work with theirs."

Even if the U.S. authorities had been able to track her to the island, they might not have gotten her back. She shoved away her barely touched breakfast.

"Did they arrest the owner of the house?" Theo asked.

Gary rubbed the back of his neck. "He's been in France

148

for the past three months and said he had no idea his house was being used."

"Did they arrest Professor Donovan?" Jessalyn asked.

"He was held overnight and has a bail hearing this morning," Gary said.

"But—" She didn't want him running around loose.

Gary held his hand up. "I know they're planning on a stipulation that he can't go near the college campus or his bail will be rescinded and he'll sit the rest of the time until trial in jail. I'm sure it will be fine."

Jessalyn hoped so. Everything seemed to be wrapped up with all the bad guys. Except... She sat straighter. "What about the man who watched me on campus? I didn't see him last night."

Theo raised his voice and glared. "What man? Jessa, you didn't tell me someone was watching you."

She squirmed. "I wasn't totally sure. I felt icky when I saw him, and it looked like he watched me, but maybe he wasn't. Sally walked with me most of the time when he was there. And another student walked with me from the parking lot."

Theo wrapped an arm around her. "Sorry I raised my voice. Gary, is there anything you can do?"

"She could look at some mug shots of Mansard's known associates."

"Hey." Jessalyn grabbed her phone from her pocket. "I have a picture of him." She scrolled through her photos. Finding the correct one, she showed the picture to Gary.

He took the phone and studied the photo. "He's vaguely familiar, but I can't place him." He hit a few buttons, and his phone dinged. He handed hers back and picked up his own. "I'm sending it to our tech guy, and I'll ask Luke to forward it to the FBI."

If the man wasn't caught with the others, surely he'd lie low. Maybe even leave the city—make a fresh criminal start somewhere else. But what if he didn't? What if the man found out she was the reason the local police got involved? Maybe he'd remember that she could identify him.

Theo clasped her hand. "I'm hiring a bodyguard to go to school with you until this guy is found. And you'll be done with this semester in a couple of weeks, anyway."

It must cost a lot for a trained bodyguard to follow someone around for six hours. Then she had work. Theo would have the bodyguard drive her to work. Surely, she'd be safe in his office building.

She gazed into Theo's eyes. "I was so scared last night." She blinked to stop the tears that misted her eyes and let out a long breath. "I know that guy might look for me on campus again, so I would feel better having someone with me, but once I'm in my classroom, I'll be fine."

Theo shook his head. "No. He'll be with you the whole school day."

She gave a decisive nod, and the knot in her stomach loosened. "Okay. I'll feel better anyway."

A chair scraped the floor and her gaze flew to Gary. Jessalyn had forgotten about him. He pointed down the hallway to the pool. "I'll go now and find my wife and kid."

Bradley stood. "Yeah, I've got stuff to do, too. Glad you're okay Jessalyn."

After they left, Theo pushed his chair back and situated her on his lap. "After you finish exams, how about we take a honeymoon?"

She lifted her eyebrows. "But I just started working at AAJ. I don't want my boss to show favoritism."

He nuzzled her neck. "You're going to quit anyway when you start your full school schedule. It'll be a little sooner."

She wrapped her arms around the back of his neck. "I suppose you're right. I would love to go on a honeymoon. And I love you." She grimaced. "Not in that order."

He laughed and kissed her.

She twined her fingers with his. "Taking a honeymoon makes it feel like we have a real marriage."

"Hey." He tipped her chin up and stared into her eyes. "Honeymoon or not, we do have a real marriage. It might have started a bit rough, but we love each other and that's what matters."

Her heart was stuffed so full, Jessalyn didn't think she could love Theo more.

He rubbed his hand up and down her back. "Now, the honeymoon. Where do you want to go?"

She shrugged. "I haven't been on a vacation since I was a preteen. Anywhere you are will be perfect."

"I'll come up with some options. This is a decision we're making together." Theo pulled out his phone. "I have to line up a bodyguard for Monday. Do you want to swim with the family after that?"

"Sure."

The reminder of the bodyguard crashed her back to reality. She hoped they'd find this guy and it would turn out he'd only been waiting for his daughter, and not there to watch her. But the creepy feeling she got when he stared at her convinced her *she* wouldn't want him for a father.

Chapter 18

Jessalyn waited in the passenger seat of her Mustang for Chris Billings, Theo's hired bodyguard, to check out the school parking lot and surrounding area. He was dressed in jeans and a T-shirt like most of the students.

He opened her door. "All set."

She swung her legs around, but didn't get out. She had a flash of Professor Donovan lecturing the class. With his gaze on her and telling them how important it was to make patients comfortable, it took on a whole new meaning.

Chris squatted in front of her. "Hey, what's wrong?"

Jessalyn drew in a shuddering breath. "I just remembered Professor Donovan. He's the one who gave us the invitations to the auction."

Chris took her hands and gave a squeeze. "He was arrested. They'll never let him on campus again."

She looked into his eyes. "I know you're right, but I guess I was hit with a waking nightmare."

He stood and she got out with her backpack and pointed. "That's the admin building. We've got time now to get your parking sticker." They hadn't used his car with the risk of it being towed, and he'd insisted on being the one to drive hers.

"I'll be more comfortable when we can use my car." His gaze constantly darted from side to side as they walked across campus and into the admin building.

"I bet mine can get us out of a sticky situation faster than yours."

He grinned. "You're probably right, but if we didn't lose them and got shot at, mine has the added protection of being bulletproof."

"Yeah. I don't want bullet holes in my new Mustang." This wasn't a hypothetical conversation. It was so unreal, like she'd been dropped into an action movie. Little, insignificant Jessalyn Waters with a bodyguard and a bulletproof car. And a billionaire husband who loved her. Her world had been turned upside down, but hopefully soon, she could enjoy the good parts.

With the new parking sticker in Chris's pocket, they entered her first classroom. Since getting the sticker took less time than expected, they arrived early. There was only one student in the room. Jessalyn started to take her usual seat in the front, when Chris touched her shoulder.

"We're sitting in back. I need eyes on everyone, and I want you to be harder to find."

"But…" She always sat in front. "Fine." They picked out seats in the middle of the back row.

Students trickled in, many eyeing Chris before taking seats—the surprising new face the last week before exams. Some of the women's gazes appraised him. He had wide shoulders and muscled arms, but Jessalyn preferred Theo's sleek swimmer's body. Professor Bradburn entered with a coffee in one hand and a satchel in the other. She set them on her desk and started rooting through the bag.

Chris leaned closer. "Be right back." He strode to the front and whispered to the professor, pulling his wallet from his back pocket. She didn't see what he did with it, but maybe he showed her some kind of bodyguard badge.

Two rows ahead, Ashley turned around. "Jessalyn, who is that?"

They hadn't discussed what to tell anyone, and did it matter if the students knew? "He's my bodyguard."

The girl's eyes widened. "Whoa. Did you marry into the mafia or something?"

Jessalyn's mouth dropped open, never expecting a mafia question. "No. I ran into some trouble over the weekend, and my husband felt more comfortable with me having personal protection."

"Were you one—"

Luckily, Professor Bradburn interrupted the conversation. "Let's get started."

Chris dropped into the seat beside her.

Jessalyn whispered. "I've got a paperback in my bag if you want to read."

His eyebrows spiked up. "I'm on duty." He leaned back, one arm resting in his lap and the other on the desk.

At the end of class, they waited for the students to file out before they left the room. He had her stay inside as he exited the building and scanned the area. There were too many students to see anyone suspicious—at least, not that she noticed, and the bench where Creeper Guy sat was empty. He waved her outside, and they strode to the next building. They entered, and Sally jumped up from a bench near the door, hurrying toward them. Chris stepped between them.

Jessalyn touched Chris's back. "Chris, it's all right. This is Sally. She was with me that night. We talked on the phone, but I haven't seen her since."

He eased aside and the women hugged.

Jessalyn stepped back. "Sally, this is Chris. He's my bodyguard until we find the guy who was watching us." She glanced at Chris. "I typically give Sally a ride home after our last class."

He nodded and glanced at the door.

Sally wiggled her fingers at him. "Hi." She grabbed Jessalyn's arm and they marched down the hall. She leaned close. "He's hot."

"He's married with kids."

Sally glanced over her shoulder. "Darn. So, how are you doing?"

Jessalyn shrugged. "Okay. The last two days, I couldn't let Theo out of my sight or I'd freak. I'm kind of glad he hired Chris. I'm not sure if I could've come to school on my own. What about you?"

"It wasn't a big deal. I mean, it was, but I didn't know I would have been swept off to a fate worse than death. I didn't feel the undercurrent at the party. After I woke up in the hospital, an FBI guy told me what happened, but it felt like he was telling me about some case not related to me. I don't think I was very helpful."

They did much the same thing in the second class as the first, although this one was huge with almost a hundred students. She never wanted a semester to be over as much as now. Between Creeper Guy watching her and having a honeymoon in a couple weeks, she was done.

Class ended, and they walked back to the first building for the last class of her day. The bench remained empty. Sally chattered as if nothing had ever happened to them. Jessalyn hoped the other women were as seemingly unaffected by the events of that night.

As they approached the classroom, Sally said, "I don't ever want to see Professor Donovan again. I can't believe he acted like we were doing other students a favor, when he was sending us to be sold off."

Jessalyn drew in a long breath, and reminded herself he wasn't there. If she ever saw him again, it would be in court.

Chris preceded them into the classroom. All the students bunched together in the front of the room, chattering in small groups. Usually, everyone took a seat upon entering.

One of the students glanced at them. "Hey, did you guys hear that Professor Donovan was arrested for trafficking female students?"

Relief washed over her that nobody knew yet who the

women were. Maybe they'd finish the semester before everyone found out. By the time the next semester started, there'd be other news to catch everyone's attention. "Um. Yeah. Hard to believe, huh?"

"All right, students, take your seats." A man who appeared to be an administrator, by the looks of his suit, tie, and white shirt, strode into the room and stood behind the desk.

Once everyone took seats and settled, the man cleared his throat. He shifted from one foot to the other, and his gaze seemed to be on the desk of the closest student. "Professor Donovan is no longer with the school. We'll be using his exam from last semester. So, don't worry. You *will* get credit for the class. I suggest you study whatever remains on the syllabus that hasn't been covered. You're dismissed until the exam."

With only two more class sessions left, it wouldn't be a hardship, but a few students grumbled on their way out of the room. The three of them waited like before, then Jessalyn preceded them toward the door.

"Jessalyn Waters? Sally Baker?" the administrator asked.

She really had to change her name. She glanced at Sally, who shrugged. "Yes?" They stopped in front of the desk.

"On behalf of the school, I'd like to give you our sincerest apology for Professor Donovan's behavior."

As if the professor had broken some etiquette rule rather than broken laws by trafficking students.

The man's mouth tightened. "We never suspected his involvement in anything like that, or he would have been dismissed long ago. You will be receiving a formal apology on behalf of the school."

"Thank you, sir."

They filed out of the room. She hadn't thought about how badly the school might be affected by the professor's involvement in trafficking his students. She didn't blame the school. Professor Donovan had probably been well vetted when they hired him. It wasn't their fault he veered into criminal territory.

Chris stopped them before exiting the building. He stepped outside, and from beside the door, Jessalyn scanned what she could see of the grounds. Sally did the same from the other side. Class had finished early, so few students roamed the campus.

Chris opened the door and held it wide. "Okay, ladies. Let's go."

As earlier, Jessalyn and Sally walked in front of Chris. At her Mustang, they split, the women going to the right side.

A man—Creeper Guy—rushed from behind a tree and grabbed Jessalyn. She screamed. He held her in front of him and started dragging her backwards.

Chris pulled out a gun and pointed it at them. Maybe it was pointed at Creeper's head, but she could see down the barrel.

"Let her go!" Chris said. "Sally, get in the car and lock the doors."

Sally yanked the car door open and dove inside. The locks clicked. At least one of them was safe.

"Do you really want me to use this?" Creeper Guy said, his voice taunting.

Something sharp pricked her neck. Her legs shook, and she would have sunk to the ground if his arm wasn't tight around her waist. "What is it?" she asked.

"It's a syringe." His voice was low beside her ear as he dragged her farther from her car. "But what's in it? Hmm. It could be a sedative to knock you out. Or maybe it's a drug that'll make your heart race so fast you'll have a heart attack. Or maybe it's a drug that will make you beg me to ravish you. He licked the side of her face.

She shivered. This was worse than the auction. That had been a vague threat. They wanted her alive to recover their costs. But now, she could die within minutes.

Chris still held his gun on them and took another step.

"Stop right there or she gets this," Creeper said.

"You don't want to kill her. She didn't send the FBI after your buddies."

"She's mine. I convinced George to give the loan to her brother, knowing I'd get her in the end."

Chris shook his head. "That loan was paid. George must have wanted her out of your reach since he sold her."

The needle jabbed her neck again. Chris's distracting wasn't helping her.

"She's mine."

Chris shifted a half step closer. "Come on. Let her go. You can't get away with her."

They stood at the edge of the sidewalk. His car was probably parked on the road another ten or so feet away. If something didn't change, they'd be gone. She'd become this obsessed guy's toy. No wonder his stare had unnerved her.

She flicked her gaze to the Mustang. Sally's face was blanched, eyes wide, and a knuckle was stuffed in her mouth.

Jessalyn's feet dragged on the cement. She stared at Chris. His eyes darted to the side. Was someone else there, ready to help Creeper Guy? He did it twice more. Maybe he wanted her to move to the left. It'd be nice to get farther from the needle that kept poking her. But maybe Creeper would follow her move and overcorrect, jabbing the needle deep and plunging the liquid into her.

They were back in the grass. She had to do it now, or too soon, Creeper would shove her into his car.

Jessalyn lunged to the left and somewhat forward. Creeper Guy's roar got cut short with the blast of a gunshot. Or maybe it was that she just couldn't hear anything beyond the ringing in her ears. She fell to the ground and a heavy weight fell on top of her, expelling all the air from her lungs.

At the third attempt of pulling in a breath, she succeeded as the weight was lifted off her.

Someone rolled her to her back, and Chris, on his knees at

her side, hovered over her. "Jessalyn, are you hurt?"

She gasped in two more breaths, and assessed her body. There were no sharp pains. Her ribs might be bruised, but that was nothing compared to what might have happened. "I'm okay. What happened?"

"As soon as you were clear, I shot him."

She started to lift her head, and he put his hand on her forehead. "Don't look," he said. "Just rest for a minute." He pulled out his phone and placed a call. He spoke low enough that she couldn't hear it over the ringing in her ears.

"Jessalyn!" *That* she could hear. Sally almost fell on her as she plopped down beside her. She grabbed Jessalyn's shoulders. "Don't ever do that to me again. I'm going to have nightmares."

"*You're* going to have nightmares?"

Sally pulled one hand away. "You're bleeding." She tried to push Jessalyn over, and Chris stopped her.

"It's not her blood."

Sally stared at her hand. "Ew. You've got dead-guy blood on you."

Jessalyn lifted her head. "He's dead?" The only thing she felt was relief. "Can I sit up now?"

Chris pocketed his phone. "Yes, but you really want to look into the parking lot and not this way."

She scrambled to a sitting position beside Sally, and they wrapped their arms around each other.

Sirens started in the distance, getting louder until they stopped behind her. Several car doors closed, then Gary squatted in front of her and took her hands. "Jessalyn, are you okay?"

"Yeah. Chris said that's not my blood." She was beginning to believe him as her body calmed down more, but she couldn't prevent a slight tremble in her arms.

"Good. I think Theo would have shot Chris if anything happened to you. I heard the call over the radio about a shooting on campus, and came in case it involved you. So, I'm not officially here."

"Can I go home now? Chris probably knows better what happened than I do." She didn't want to relive it by telling them about it. The ringing in her ears had reduced by half.

Gary patted her knee. "Sorry. They'll want to talk to you."

Two uniformed officers stepped in front of them. "Jessalyn Argyle?" the one with curly hair and gray eyes asked.

"That's me."

He squatted in front of her and the other officer pulled Sally up and they stepped away from them. "I'm Officer McDonald. Can you tell me what happened?"

Jessalyn closed her eyes and drew in a long breath, then explained the incident.

He leaned toward her. "I guess he did poke you."

"What?" Her hand flew to her neck. "Ouch." She pulled her fingers away. They were sticky with blood. "I'm bleeding."

"It's just a little bit, but you should probably clean it with disinfectant."

There was a commotion behind her and she started to turn.

"You don't want to look," Officer McDonald said.

Then there was the rasp of a long zipper. She shivered. They could have been bagging her if Creeper Guy really had that one drug in the syringe and used it.

"You done, Terry?" Gary asked.

"For now."

Gary helped Jessalyn up. "Chris, do you have any idea how long you'll be?"

Chris shrugged. "I shot someone, so who knows."

"All right. Bring Jessalyn's car when you're done. I'm going to take the girls home."

"My backpack!" No way could she lose it days before exams.

160

"I'll get it." Sally hurried to the car and picked Jessalyn's bag off the ground and retrieved her own from inside.

They walked to Gary's car, and Jessalyn pulled at her shirt. "I can't get blood in your car."

Gary shook his head. "I'll get a towel from my gym bag."

He got the towel and wrapped it around her shoulders. "Let's go."

Jessalyn climbed into the front passenger seat and buckled in. She leaned back and relaxed her shoulders. It had to be over now.

Chapter 19

The family gathered around the dining table, the meal finished and plates pushed away. It was the first Friday Theo had eaten at home in months. There was no need to head to Zentarro's to see Jessa when she sat right beside him. He took her hand under the table and smiled at her. She'd been through some pretty scary stuff and had relaxed after Jimmy Harper's death on campus Monday.

He kissed Jessa's cheek then turned to Gary, who sat at the head of the table. Once Susan, Autumn, and Gary moved in another month, Theo would sit at the head. He hadn't wanted to fill his father's place there, but was ready now. With a wife and maybe a baby by the end of next year, it was time. "All right, Gary, fill us in."

Gary's gaze traveled around the table. "Autumn, maybe you should do some homework."

"Aw, Gary. I did all my homework before dinner." She crossed her arms. "I know what's going on, anyway."

They'd told Autumn some of the facts, but not the nasty ones. Theo didn't know how much Gary would be revealing. He was very protective of his stepdaughter.

Susan stood. "Autumn, let's go for a swim."

"Mom." She stretched out the one word, Theo held back a grin.

"You want to pass up swimming?"

Autumn studied each face, and must have decided she wasn't getting any more information. "All right."

After they climbed the stairs, Gary cleared his throat. "I'll start with Jimmy Harper. He was George Mansard's cousin. Besides the syringe he held to Jessalyn's neck, the police found another in his pocket. They contained a sedative."

Jessa's hand twitched in his, and Theo gave it a squeeze, then scooted her chair closer and dropped his arm around her shoulders. If Chris hadn't been with Jessa, she might have disappeared. She was finally safe.

"And yesterday." Gary stopped as Autumn's voice came closer, then faded as she and Susan headed to the pool. "Authorities raided Victor Cortez's island. They brought six women back to the states and ten others to various other countries. Cortez should get a long sentence with so many testifying against him."

It was a relief the other women had been freed. Even more so that Jessa hadn't been taken there and suffered while waiting for rescue. If the man had gotten away, would the FBI have known where to look? There were so many women Mansard and the others had taken. He hoped the FBI could track down more of them, but was sure some would never find their way home.

Theo shifted his chair back and hauled Jessa onto his lap. Her eyebrows shot up.

He hugged her. "I am so, so glad you're here and safe."

She buried her face in his neck. "Me, too. There's nowhere I'd rather be."

"Anyway," Gary said, "the FBI is pleased with the round-up." He stood. "I'll go check on Susan and Autumn."

Bradley shook his head. "I can't believe all this happened right here. Jessalyn, you are one lucky chick."

She kissed Theo's cheek. "Don't I know it? Theo's my hero."

Bradley chuckled. "Well, I hope this isn't some kind of

trend. First Gary rescues Susan, now Theo rescues you. I don't want a woman that bad."

"Hey, Bradley. I have a favor to ask. Jessalyn and I are going on a honeymoon after she takes her exams. I'd like you to step in as CEO while I'm gone."

"How long is this honeymoon going to be?"

Theo shrugged. "A couple of weeks? Maybe longer if we're having fun."

Bradley laughed. "Aren't honeymoons supposed to be fun?"

Jessa ducked her head and blushed. Theo would make sure they had lots of that kind of fun.

"So, will you do it?" Theo asked. "You can call me every couple days with questions. Just don't go too overboard lording it over everybody." Theo knew he wouldn't. Bradley was a successful, well liked head of his division.

"Sure." He stood and leaned his hands on the table. "But if I like it, you might have to fight me for control when you get back."

Theo winked at Jessa. "Thanks, bro."

Bradley patted Theo's shoulder on the way out.

The doorbell rang.

"I've got it," Bradley called out.

Voices murmured and Bradley appeared in the doorway. "Jessalyn, is this your brother?"

Mitch hovered in the doorway beside Bradley. Jessa stiffened.

Theo whispered. "I can tell him to leave if you want."

She drew in a long breath. "No, let him come in."

Theo waved across the table. "Mitch, have a seat." Without taking his gaze off the man, he called out. "Go away, Bradley."

He grinned. "Man, I thought you'd forget I was here."

The siblings silently stared at each other until Bradley's footsteps retreated up the stairs.

Theo shifted Jessa so she faced Mitch, but didn't let her go. "What brings you here, Mitch?"

Mitch's gaze darted between him and Jessa. "Um. I saw on the news that Mansard was arrested in a trafficking ring raid."

"That's right," Theo said. One Jessa should never have been involved in.

Jessa remained stiff in his arms. Theo wished she didn't have to relive one of the most painful times in her life.

Mitch twisted his hands on the table and kept his focus on them. "It drove home that because of me, one of those auctioned girls could have been Jess."

Theo tightened his arms around her. "Jessalyn *was* one of those women auctioned."

Mitch's eyes widened, and he gasped.

"I almost didn't get her back." His throat clogged and he swallowed.

Jessa leaned back into him.

Mitch stretched his arms out in front of him, palms up. "Jess, I am so sorry I put you through this." He pulled a check out of his shirt pocket and unfolded it, sliding it to the center of the table. "I came to buy you back."

The amount of the check was a hundred-sixty thousand.

Jessa spoke for the first time. "Did you find another loan shark? Did you put me up for collateral again?"

"No, Jess. I would never do that again. I sold my design. This is half the money. And I still own a share of it. I wanted you to have a choice this time."

Jessa picked up the check and raised her eyebrows at Theo.

"Baby, this was never about the money. You keep it or give it back. It's your decision."

She kissed his cheek and tore the check in half, stacked the pieces and tore it again, and again until she couldn't tear it. Then she held her hand a foot above the table and released the confetti, letting it snow down onto the surface.

Theo grinned. "That was the best money I ever spent."

Mitch's mouth had dropped open. "So, Jess, you're okay being with him?"

She leaned into Theo and he tightened his arm around her. "We're married, and I love him. We're taking a honeymoon after I finish my exams." She pointed a finger at her brother. "This doesn't atone for what you did. I still haven't forgiven you, but I'm not angry anymore."

His shoulders dropped and he blew out a breath. "Okay. I can live with that. One step at a time. Jess, I really am sorry. Thank you, Theo, for stepping in to do my job to save her." He stood and circled around the table. "Jess, can I hug you?"

Theo couldn't guess which way she'd go on that.

Finally, she stood, and Mitch wrapped his arms around her. "I've missed you, Jess. I-I hope you'll see me again."

She stepped back, and Theo stood, putting an arm around her waist. "I'll call you after we get back. Maybe we can meet for lunch."

They walked to the door and Theo opened it.

Mitch turned back. "You've got yourself a good man, Jess. I'm leaving you in the best of hands."

"I know. Bye, Mitch."

Theo closed the door and put his back to it. He pulled Jessa into him. "I love you. Despite what Mitch did that threw us together, we still would have ended up married. But it might have taken longer. Probably a lot longer."

Jessa smiled and his heart flipped. He'd almost lost her. It would take a while to not be compelled to keep checking on her.

She pushed up, sliding her body against his, turning his mind to other needs.

Her fingers rubbed his neck. "You mean, if you'd had a chance to ask me on that date, we wouldn't have ended up married by the end of it?"

He chuckled. "Not even close. But I've got you now, and

I'm not letting go."

"Good." She stepped back, grabbed his hand and dragged him toward the stairs. She glanced over her shoulder and pursed her lips. "I have some naughty plans for you."

"I like where this is going." He scooped her up and sped up the stairs. He would cherish every moment with her, always remembering how fate had worked in their favor.

The End

About **Her Choice** – Book 4 in the Choice Series by Deborah Wallace

He's falling for his sister-in-law while under suspicion for his wife's murder.

The best day of Bradley Argyle's life is the day his son is born. It's also his worst day. His wife is murdered in her hospital bed, and he's the prime suspect.

Then she shows up.

His wife's identical twin sister. Except they aren't alike in any way that matters. Peyton is sunny and caring, while her sister had been cold and rejected their baby.

Peyton Quinn is devastated when she arrives at the hospital to find out her estranged sister was married, had a baby, and is now dead. She accepts Bradley's offer to become the baby's nanny and quickly falls for her nephew. Then Bradley is arrested for her sister's murder, but not before she realizes she's fallen for him as well.

To have a future, they'll have to dig up her sister's dark secrets to find her killer.

Books by Deborah Wallace

Wounded Warrior Hearts Series (Clean Romance)
Wounded Warrior Hearts: Steven
Wounded Warrior Hearts: Amy
Wounded Warrior Hearts: Russ

Rawlins Series (Paranormal Romance – witches)
Kathleen's Legacy
Jason's Forbidden Woman
Jamie's Trials
Adam's Redemption
Kristy's Puzzle
Tony's to Protect
Abby's Salem Legacy
Keith's Return
Gabe's Atonement – *December 2024*

Choice Series (Romantic Suspense)
Second Choice
Third Choice
No Choice
Her Choice
Series Complete

Unknown Series (Romantic Suspense)
Father Unknown
Killer Unknown
Series Complete

Other Books (Romantic Suspense)
I Shot the Sheriff
Your Love Belongs to Me

New Memories – Receive this book free by signing up for my newsletter on my website.

Check out my website for details on these books and where to find them. You can also sign up to receive emails when I have a new book. www.DeborahWallaceBooks.com.

Or find my books on Amazon:
https://www.amazon.com/Deborah-Wallace/e/B07XDL4X89

About Deborah Wallace

Deborah Wallace decided to try writing what she liked to read, and stories started filling her head. Writing has become a passion, and she can't go long without touching her keyboard.

She's written in different genres, but the stories she keeps coming back to are her favorite—romantic suspense. The first *Rawlins* book was supposed to be the only paranormal. Then she asked 'what if…' and now children of the first characters and a couple of friends have books.

She wrote her first stories in 2014 but didn't publish until 2019.

Deborah grew up in Michigan, but Massachusetts has been her home for more years than she cares to think about. She loves the history, the museums and antique houses, the seacoast and hiking trails.

www.ingramcontent.com/pod-product-compliance
Lightning Source LLC
Chambersburg PA
CBHW020128180626
46810CB00004B/1456